THE APPLE ORCHARD
BED & BREAKFAST

THE APPLE ORCHARD BED & BREAKFAST

RON AND CARYL MCADOO

Five Star • Waterville, Maine

Five Star First Edition Romance Series.

Published in 2002 in conjunction with
Cherry Weiner Literary Agency.

Set in 11 pt. Plantin by Rick Gundberg.

Printed in the United States on permanent paper.

Library of Congress Cataloging-in-Publication Data

McAdoo, Ron.
   The Apple Orchard Bed and Breakfast / Ron and
Caryl McAdoo.
      p. cm. (Five Star First Edition Romance Series)
      ISBN 0-7862-4234-5 (hc : alk. paper)
      1. Bed and breakfast accommodations—Fiction. 2. Rich
people—Fiction. 3. Recluses—Fiction. 4. Widows—
Fiction. 5. Texas—Fiction. 6. Love stories. I. Title.
Series: Five Star first edition romance series
Gsafd Other authors: McAdoo, Caryl.
PS3613.C26A87 2002
   813'.6—21   2002022885

Dedication

Love never fails. It is not envious or boastful, nor does it demand its own way. Love is patient and kind, never remembers wrongs suffered, and rejoices in the truth.

It bears, believes, and hopes all this. We are blessed by the forever love we've found together.

Acknowledgements

We thank God for the talents and many blessings He's given us. We recognize that all good things come from Him, and that apart from Him, we are nothing.

A big thanks to the DFW Writers' Workshop for their support and mentoring these past ten years—
especially John, Jack, and Don.

Our appreciation to another Workshop colleague and friend, Linda, who helped make this work the best it could be before it left Texas.

Thanks Hazel for the wonderful suggestions. We love you being our editor.

You all are blessings.

INTER-OFFICE MEMO

To: Senior Personnel Counselors

- A well-to-do widower, somewhat of a recluse, is contemplating opening his Bed & Breakfast. He wants no preconceived ideas as to the daily operations of a B&B. Consequently, he is only interested in non-professional applicants for the position of live-in manager.

- He prefers someone of mature age, but will consider any qualified person.

- Ads will begin this Thursday in major newspapers across the country. Be prepared. We're not the only agency he's hired, and we definitely want to fill this position.

- Forward prospective applicant's files with photographs to the Post Office Box listed below. Travel vouchers will be issued to any candidate chosen for an interview.

CHAPTER ONE

Journal entry—January 31st

Another day wasted. This could be the worst idea I've ever had. On the other hand, I talked to more women just this afternoon than in the last five years. Got to admit I enjoyed them, especially how they smell. Been a long time.

She could still forget it all—not go—but she wanted to. No. She needed to go, needed to change her life. The grandfather clock struck the half-hour. The moment of decision arrived, and she couldn't put it off any longer. Marge marked her place in her paperback and retrieved the classifieds from beneath her chair. Armed with the coffee-stained paper, she faced her daughter. The words stuck to the roof of her dry mouth, held in place by her paralyzed tongue.

"Can I borrow the car this morning?"

"Where're you going?"

"To Canton. I've got a job interview."

Stephanie dropped the shirt she'd been sewing a button on. "You've got what?"

"You heard me. I called about a job, and I have an interview set up later this morning." Marge held out the paper to her daughter with the ad circled in red ink.

"B and B? What, Mother? Bridge and Bunko?"

"Oh, Stephanie, a bed and breakfast, of course. Can I

borrow your car? Or should I call a cab?" She tossed the newspaper on the coffee table, then walked from the den to the kitchen where she thumbed through the phone book.

"Wait a minute, Mom. A taxi all the way to Canton will cost you a fortune." The younger woman followed her then closed the Yellow Pages. "Would you explain why you want to get a job? I thought you were happy here?"

"Honey, it's been over five years since Daddy died." She looked out the window. The mention of Walter unsettled something inside. She pushed his memory away. "I need to get on with my life."

"But you have a life here, don't you?"

"Well, sure—as housekeeper, cook, and babysitter." She looked away and wished she could take back the part about the little ones. She loved her grandchildren, but Stephanie and Wayne left them with her more and more and thanked her less and less.

"That's not fair." Her daughter turned away and busied herself at the sink. "I do as much as you around the house, and I can't believe you'd say anything about watching the kids. I thought you enjoyed it."

"Oh, sweetheart, you know I do. I love my babies with all my heart, but I need some time to myself. Everybody does." Marge shook her head. "If you or Wayne order pizza delivered, you count that your night for cooking, and you know good and well our ideas of clean have never even been close."

"I can't believe we're having this conversation. What's got into you, Mother?" Stephanie flipped the dishtowel. "It's ridiculous. You don't know the first thing about running a bed and breakfast. What makes you think they'd hire you? Besides, your place is here with your family, not off with strangers."

"Number one, I've already interviewed with a personnel

counselor. They're not looking for experience, and there's an accounting firm that keeps the books. They want to train the manager their way. Number two, the owner wants the B&B run like a home, not a hotel. And number three, why would you think I belonged here? I'm a grown woman. I've raised my children."

Her daughter dried her hands then refilled her coffee cup. "Your room? Are you forgetting the room we added on just for you?"

Marge shook her head. "No, I certainly am not. Neither have I forgotten that it was my money that paid the bill. It's not like I'll be taking it with me. My room will be here when I come to visit."

"Oh, Mother, please. I'm sorry you're so used and abused."

"Now don't you 'Oh, Mother' me." Marge glared, but her daughter looked away.

Stephanie pouted back into the den and retrieved the paper, studying the circled ad. "Why this one? If you've got to have a job, why not find something here, something closer to home where you can still live with us?"

"It's been twenty years since I've worked. What do you think I'd be qualified for besides passing out Grandy's sugar and cream or saying good-bye to Sam's shoppers? The whole idea of a bed and breakfast intrigues me. Tell the truth. Don't you think it sounds fun? And aside from the accounting, I believe I could run one just fine."

"Well, I don't like it."

Marge smiled at the expression on her daughter's face. "Like I said, it's time for me to get on with my life. Can I borrow the car or not?"

Stephanie finally relented and gave over the keys. It amused Marge how their rolls had reversed, but she didn't like it. If this job didn't pan out, she'd find something else—no matter what anyone thought.

With one hand on the map and the other on the steering wheel, she drove the borrowed Maxima through the East Texas countryside. At the intersection, she slowed to read the sign then swung the car west on FM 1388.

Checking her scribbled instructions and the odometer, she drove straight to The Apple Orchard Bed and Breakfast without a hitch. On either side of the drive, native rocks formed curved half walls with untended flower beds at their base. Instead of daffodils or pansies common to Texas Februarys, brown ghosts of seasons past filled the beds with a few mounds of wild green clover. The entrance could certainly stand some sprucing up, and she loved to garden.

She drove past two red cedar cabins. After the second, the trail—one certainly couldn't call it a road—curved around a stand of live oaks. Berry bushes bordered one side of the winding drive, though of what variety she had no idea. Her speedometer barely registered as she inched along drinking in the sights. A quiver of excitement ran up her spine, and she smiled in spite of the butterflies tap dancing on the rock lodged in the pit of her stomach.

The neighbor to the east ran a modest herd of cattle and maintained beautifully manicured pastures, fenced and cross fenced. She appreciated the contentment grazing cows added to the tranquil scene. Dense woods grew to the west. She wondered where the apple trees were and what grew up the rows of wire trellises she passed.

Pulling to a stop on the wide circle at the end of the drive, she killed the motor and tried to still the butterflies with alternating deep breaths and dry swallows. The expanse of the rustic tin roof indicated a huge house. Oh, how wonderful it must sound under that roof during a spring shower. She closed her eyes and imagined the pitter-patter of raindrops dancing on the metal.

A Mexican man with sheepish eyes met her as she climbed the rock steps toward the porch. *"Buenos dias, señora."* He flashed a quick smile then looked immediately back to the ground, motioning for her to follow. *"Por favor."*

When she rounded the corner to the right, the porch widened, and she realized she had approached the house from its side. Twin porch swings bordered the antique double entry doors, and she couldn't resist. Sitting in the closest, she gave a little push-off with her toe and looked toward the brown man who waited by the opened door.

"My grandmother had a porch swing like this."

He held up a finger. *"Un momento, señora."* He disappeared into the house but soon returned carrying an application on a clipboard with a pen.

"My name is Marge." She patted her chest with her fingers and repeated, "Marge."

The man smiled and nodded shyly. *"Mi nombre es Jorje."* He pulled an envelope from his shirt pocket then handed it to her. "For your travel."

"Thank you, Jorje. *Gracias.*"

"Por nada." He ducked back into the house.

Before she finished the two-page questionnaire, she sensed being watched, but resisted the urge to look.

"Mrs. Winters?"

She glanced over to see a large man blocking the doorway. His face appeared weathered, but handsomely rugged. She guessed him to be around her age, late forties, maybe early fifties. It flat wasn't fair that men aged so much better than women. He seemed hard, but a smile might soften him up some.

"Yes?" She shouldn't dislike him just because he didn't show his age. "Good morning. I'm not quite finished here. Are you Mr. Preston?"

He nodded once and stepped aside. "Please, come in."

She rose, gathered her purse and sweater, then cleared her throat. Something about him eroded her confidence. Her voice quivered as she repeated, "My grandmother had a porch swing I loved." She touched her throat and swallowed. "But that was a long time ago." Why was she suddenly so nervous?

The entry's twenty-foot ceilings amplified the long and narrow dimensions of the unusual room. On the left, the wall showcased a large false window with green shutters. Ceiling-to-floor bookshelves on either side bulged with old books, and a piano beneath the faux window finished the quaint setting.

Nestled between that area and the next, a long hall with several closed doors turned off to the left. As she passed through the second area—an antique sitting arrangement—the aroma of coffee drifted from the kitchen on her right.

"This floor here came out of a skating rink in Monroe, Louisiana where my wife used to skate when she was a little girl." Mr. Preston chuckled. "Made a mistake trying to salvage a piece from the corner section. Took forever to get it sanded down and installed."

"Oh, how unique! That's so interesting! I'm sure your wife appreciates all your trouble."

"She did. She's dead now."

"I'm sorry."

Preston pointed to a door on the right at the end of the room, allowing her to walk ahead. "My office is through there."

She wanted to turn and enjoy a closer inspection of the curious hall, but instead, breezed past him toward the back. Hundreds of glass panes in old windows mounted side by side created the end wall, allowing a spacious view across a screened porch to the back yard. A calico cat leapt high into the air with her paws spread playing with a gray tabby. Paned French doors led to the porch, and she wanted to investigate, but turned right, following his directions to step into a warm, masculine room. Embers glowed in the fireplace.

Preston motioned to a wing-backed chair and remained standing while Marge seated herself, then went around behind a large desk and leaned on his worn leather chair.

"How about a cup of coffee?"

"Why, thank you. I'd love a cup even if I usually don't drink it this late in the day. It smelled so good when we came through."

She smiled as he left then returned to the questions on the application. Her cheeks grew warm when some of the information seemed more personal than business related, but she'd never applied for such a position.

Did she have any tattoos? Well, she never!

And why would he need to know the ages of her children and grandchildren's names and ages? A bit of disgust at her ignorance of what was permissible chided her, but she chose to excuse much of it because of the unusual situation. After all, she would be living here. Hmm. Would Preston, too? That might be a problem. Maybe he lived in one of those cabins she passed on the two-lane trail coming in. Surely he wouldn't expect—

Preston returned, and she accepted the steaming cup as she handed him the clipboard. While he sat down and examined the application, she sipped her coffee and studied him. Fifty, at least. Hmm, he moved his lips as he read, but not a lot.

13

Preston looked up. "You're a widow and have no dependent children?"

"Yes, that's right, but there's something I'd like you to know, Mr. Preston, before we proceed any further. I left a question blank there. I don't see that it's any of your business whether or not I have a tattoo."

He leaned back, but his eyes never left hers. She stared back until he laughed.

"You're absolutely right. You don't have to answer that question. I shouldn't have had it on there. Please, forgive me."

"Of course."

He scooted his chair forward, focused on her answers a minute, then looked up. "So how long's it been since your husband's death?"

"Five years since my Walter passed."

"Interesting." He turned his eyes back to the form and continued reading.

She wanted to know why her husband being dead five years was interesting, but thought it best to let him ask the questions for the time being. Her focus turned to the room. Old weathered pine covered the walls. Brick showed through some of the knotholes on the wall shared with the kitchen. And it had a window in it. How odd, a window on an inside wall. Hmm. Before she completed her inspection, he cleared his throat.

"How does four thousand a month plus room and board sound?"

"Four thousand? Well, it sounds great, but—" She paused. "Well, I guess you can see there that I've never managed a bed and breakfast. You do understand that?"

"Just the way I wanted. Nothing to it, really. Just treat the guests like family and treat me like a guest."

14

So he would be there.

He stood and walked around facing her. "Want the job?"

She gazed out the far windows to the woods and took a deep breath. "Yes. I'd love to have it. When do you want me to start?"

He ignored her question and handed her a folded piece of paper. "Now that I've hired you, here's your first bonus."

"Bonus?" She examined the check, the equivalent of a month's salary. "But I haven't earned a bonus, Mr. Preston. And this seems far too generous."

He picked a legal-sized document off his desk and extended it toward her. "Sign this, and you have."

"Well, I guess I have heard of a signing bonus." She read, then unsure, re-read the text. "If I'm correct, I'm agreeing not to divulge anything of what you're about to tell me. Is that all it says, or am I missing something?"

"Nope, that's about it."

She signed then slipped the check into her purse. She'd do some shopping on her way home and pick up a few gifts for the children.

"My ad's a bit deceiving, Mrs. Winters. I don't intend to open the bed and breakfast anytime soon. Actually, what I'm after is a wife."

A tingling sensation burned her cheeks as blood rushed upwards. She always hated the way she blushed so easily and knew from the heat, her face must be crimson. "I'm afraid I don't understand." She fidgeted and scooted to the edge of her seat. "Why do you want to hire me?"

"My wife died five years ago last month. Since that time, I haven't left the property." He walked over to the window and stared out. "I don't want to go lookin' for a wife, so I hit on this idea." He shrugged and turned back toward her. "Seemed like a good one. Anyway, you're my fifty-first applicant." He rubbed his upper lip, partially covering his mouth. "So far, I've employed seven of those women, and hopefully you'll agree to be the eighth."

"I'm sorry, but I still don't understand. You've already employed seven women? Employed them to do what, Mr. Preston? If you're not opening, then what exactly is the position you're hiring for?" She found herself fascinated by this eccentric man and his wonderful old house.

"You could say I'm hiring you to be yourself. If you're a cleaner, clean. If you like to cook, cook. Or if you're a prima donna, then sit on your donna and order the other women around." He grinned.

She cocked her head and mustered a weak smile. "May I ask why you chose me?"

He stared at her for a second then shrugged. "I like the way you smell." He moved to the chair next to her, sat, and clasped his hands, elbows resting on his knees. "You've been a widow as long as I've been a widower. Thought that was an interesting coincidence. You don't have young children. There're a few other reasons. Will you stay?"

His easy manner, rugged looks, and deep, resonant voice appealed to her, but she had come looking for a job.

"Mr. Preston . . ." She mentally rehearsed the right words then looked him square in the eye. "You don't expect any of these women . . . uh . . . to sleep with you, do you?"

"Heavens, no. I certainly do not." He smiled. "I don't buy sex, Mrs. Winters. Could be, I'll figure this is a ridiculous way to try and find a wife, but living with eight woman should at least give me an idea of what I'm getting myself into. What do you say?"

"I don't know." She stood and turned away. "Oh Lord, what should I do?" she whispered to herself. "You haven't been out of your house in five years?"

"Oh, yes. I get out of the house. I manage a business from here, have an apple orchard. I haven't been off my property. Hadn't had any reason." He held his hands out palms up. "Got delivery trucks and UPS. Everything I need right here. Even got a doctor who makes house calls." He brought his hands together and in one graceful swoop lowered them to his lap and leaned forward. "I'm offering a six-month guarantee."

How could she not like this man? He seemed genuine and down to earth. If all he wanted was to pay for her time while he got to know her, she'd be a fool not to take it. She'd have seven other women as chaperones. It wouldn't be like she was living here alone with him. If nothing else, she could use the time to find another job.

"Am I obligating myself for the entire six months?"

"Oh, no, it's not like you're going to be an indentured servant or anything. You can leave whenever you want."

"So, you're not looking for a manager for your bed and breakfast at all?" He shook his head. "Are you ever going to open it?"

"Yeah, maybe, someday. Nancy, that's my wife, she wanted one real bad. Thought it would be a great way to meet interesting folks from all over the country. But I don't eat breakfast, so it may have to be a bed and bath. Who knows?"

She hesitated a moment longer then extended her right hand. "When would you like me to start?"

Preston jumped to his feet and clasped it with a firm grip. "Everyone's to be here at seven a.m. sharp. First day of March."

"First of March it is." She turned to leave.

"Oh, one last thing." Preston handed her a slip of paper. "You'll need to call this number to make an appointment for a physical sometime before the first."

"No problem, I'll be happy to." With plenty to think about, she started out, but halfway down the hall, stopped, then decided to wait until she came back to ask about the apple trees.

CHAPTER TWO

Journal entry—March 1st

Let the games begin. Everyone came in this morning. Got all my ladies together.

The phone rang. Instead of answering, Vicki incorporated the bell into her dream. It rang again. The third piercing trill stirred her enough to lift the receiver. Who had been on the phone in her dream? She couldn't recall.

"What?" Forcing her eyes open, she focused several times on the glowing digital numbers across her hotel room. Augggh, four in the morning. The fancy hotel's recorded message rattled in her ear. "Okay, okay." She fumbled the phone back into its cradle and rolled out of bed. "Three hours sleep? Good grief, I've got to be crazy."

Forty-five minutes later, she walked into a deserted lobby, returned her key card to the front desk, then staggered past the waterfalls to the dazzling main entrance. With a last look around, she spoke aloud to herself, "I always wanted a stay at the Hyatt Regency. Thank you, Mr. Preston." She pushed once on the revolving door.

The doorman met her on the other side and took her bag. "Transportation?"

"Taxi, please."

He blew two musical notes on the high-pitched whistle

that hung around his neck.

"Find out how much the fare will be to Canton."

"Oh, it's not far. What hundred block, ma'am?" He set her bag near the front curb.

"No, the city. The place where they have First Monday. You know, in East Texas. That Canton."

The cab whizzed around the drive and stopped with his rear bumper beside her bag. The driver leaned across the front seat and popped the trunk lid.

Just like the concierge had promised, a taxi anytime, day or night at the Hyatt. She watched as the hotel's uniformed doorman opened the back door, then leaned in to speak to the cabby. Woo hoo. She admired his cute derriere and wondered when a boy became a man.

He stepped aside. "The driver said it shouldn't run over a hundred, but he'll have to charge whatever the meter reads."

She pressed a folded bill into the doorman's hand before sliding into the back seat and speaking to her driver. "The place I'm going is about fifteen miles out of Canton, and I've *got* to be there no later than seven."

"No problem, lady."

While the doorman placed her bags in the trunk, she took one last look at the gold and glass building she always fantasized to be the castle of a fairy princess, but the ungodly hour ruined any chance of her feeling like that princess this morning. The strong mix of incense and foul body odor inside the taxi nixed any fantasy of a fairytale. She leaned her head back against the seat.

"You know I-20 to Canton, right? I'll tell you where to go from there."

She stayed awake while the man maneuvered his cab through the empty streets of downtown Dallas, but once he reached the maze of intersecting highways, she allowed herself the luxury of dreaming about a life with Mr. W. G. Preston. She reflected on what grand and glorious things a girl could do with his kind of money.

She searched for her favorite mental picture of Mr. Preston. Almost a month had passed since she'd seen him in person, and the newspaper pictures didn't due him justice, though he was a looker in his younger years, too. Wonder if he found anyone else to take the deal. The driver hit the brakes causing her to open her eyes with a start. Soon as the oncoming car passed, the cab whipped around an eighteen-wheeler, and she returned to her thoughts. Maybe Preston stopped looking after she accepted.

Pulling a mirror out of her handbag, she checked her reflection. One thing for sure. If the man likes young and beautiful, he need look no further. She threw a puckered kiss to her faintly lit image.

She dozed as the driver sped through the countryside. When he stopped for gas in Canton and she noticed the time, her shoulder and neck muscles knotted. She rolled down her window and stuck her head out. "Didn't you say you'd have no problem getting me there by seven?"

"We're here, lady." He checked his watch. "With almost twenty minutes to spare."

"And I told you the place is fifteen miles out of the city proper."

He shrugged. "So, you're a few minutes late."

"No! I can't be late. If you expect any tip at all, you best get your ass back in the driver's seat. I mean now! Pump gas on your own time."

The man paid for the fuel and jumped in the car. "Okay, okay. Where to?"

She gave him the directions. "It's an extra fifty if you get me there before seven."

"Yes, ma'am." The sedan screeched out of the station, knocking her against the back seat.

Why didn't she leave earlier or stay closer? The last thing she wanted to do was screw up her opportunity to marry money.

She pulled herself to the edge of the seat and leaned over the front. The cabby whipped around a station wagon, barely beating the oncoming traffic. She rolled her head and stretched her shoulders.

"The turn-off will jump up on you if you're not careful." She bit her lip to keep from telling him to slow down. "It's Farm-to-Market 1388."

"Got it, lady."

When the cabby turned into the entrance of the B&B, Vicki's watch read four minutes till. She fished two one-hundred-dollar bills from her purse and dropped them over the seat.

"Easy come, easy go!" She gathered the last of her things as he pulled to a stop. The dust cloud continued beyond the car and almost choked her as she hollered on her way to the house, "Keep the change!" She spit and coughed.

Vicki dropped her shoulder bag in the hall and joined seven women sitting at a montage of kitchen tables. A quick scan revealed no W. G. Preston. The other women sipped coffee and glanced around, but for all practical purposes, the room remained eerily silent considering all the hens present. Pretty unusual. The knots in her shoulders eased, and she sank into the closest empty chair at a table with only one middle-aged woman. So where was the rooster, anyway? She checked her watch again.

"Excuse me, lady. Where did you want this bag?" The taxi driver stood in the doorway.

"Oh, thanks. I almost forgot. Just set it there." With her elbows on the table, she supported her face with both hands. "I sure hope Preston doesn't expect us to get up this early every day or I'm outta here."

The blonde across from her shook her head then stuck out her hand. "I'm Audrey McLaudin. Are you all right? Because you look terrible!" She tossed her honey-colored tresses behind her shoulder.

What a witch. Vicki grinned. "Wild livin', I guess. Spent the last thou of Mr. Preston's signing bonus on one last fling." Not much competition here she mused. But that hair! Only three year olds have that color naturally. Had to come out of a bottle.

Audrey opened her mouth, but the rooster crowed before she could offer any response.

"Ladies, good morning. Glad each of you decided to take me up on my offer." He walked around the long serving counter and poured himself a mug of coffee.

"First," he took a sip, "I want you to understand this is not a contest. And there are no guarantees, either given or asked for." Sitting his coffee down, he looked around the room and stopped with a nod or smile to each woman as he continued. "There are eight rooms available, six downstairs and two up. The first order of business is to settle yourselves in. Choose a room and get unpacked."

A dark-haired woman with a silver-white skunk streak set just off center spoke up. "But how do we decide who gets what room? I, for one, don't particularly want to be upstairs."

"Dorothy, isn't it? Sorry, I forget your last name." He pointed toward the heavy-set woman who had obviously been a beauty in her younger years.

"Casey."

"Right." He nodded. "I don't care how y'all decide. Stake a claim, then fight it out if anyone tries to jump your digs."

He drained his coffee and walked toward the door. "My office is off limits. If you need anything, ask Jorje or catch me at lunch.

"Have a good morning, ladies, and I'll see you at noon, that is, if anyone wants to cook." A slight grin eased across his lips.

Vicki jumped up, fetched her bags, and raced down the side hall. From her first visit, she knew exactly which room she wanted, the last one downstairs on the right. The biggest, of course, even had its own kitchen, not that she'd be using it much. But she liked that room's decor the best—a crisp white with lots of bright primary-colored accents. Plus it had a huge Jacuzzi.

She unpacked her clothes, arranged her toilet items, then took a bath. The tiny jets pulsed, and the hot water massaged away the last of her tension. She closed her eyes. "Oh, man, I'm going to love this deal." Counting room and board in with her salary, she figured about five grand a month—and for doing nothing but being her glorious self. She hugged her shoulders and squealed.

After the bath, she wrapped in a towel and fell on her bed. Within minutes, her mind drifted to a peaceful slumber.

A double knock woke her. The door creaked open, and the heavy-set loud mouth stuck her skunk head into the room. "You Vicki?"

She opened her eyes and looked at her clock. A two-hour nap. That's what she called being herself all right. "Yeah, that'd be me." She rolled onto her side and propped her head with a pillow.

The nap-buster barged in with another old woman Vicki hadn't met close behind. "Some of us ladies have been working on a cooking schedule. You know?" She flashed her list as though Vicki could read it.

The other one spoke up. "Which meal do you want, honey?"

"Sorry, I don't cook. And I really don't care much for other women calling me honey, either." She stretched.

Miss Organizer studied her clipboard. "Oh, well, I guess you could always swap with someone. They can cook for you, and you could do their dishes, you know. Would you prefer breakfast, lunch, or dinner?"

Vicki raised one eyebrow. The way this woman talked with her hands amused her, but she had another think coming if she thought she could assign her any work. Who died and made her Hitler anyway? "I'm not sure I caught your name."

"Dorothy Casey."

"Well, Dorothy." She spread her fingers, admired her sculptured nails, then wiggled them in Chub's direction. "I don't do dishes, either. The nails, you know."

The woman jammed her hands on her hips and straightened her back. "Fine. Guess you won't eat, either, then."

"Look. I don't think that's up to you. I'm just not into domestic. If you ladies choose to cook, that'll be just great with me because I *am* into eating. Though obviously not quite as much as some people."

Chub's face flamed bright red. She took one step forward then turned on her heels and stormed out of the room. Vicki laughed into her pillow. "What a cow! Why would Preston ever have asked her to stay anyway?"

"That's not being very nice now, is it?"

Vicki lowered the feather pillow. The second softer looking lady remained. Dark hair salted with glistening silver even in the dim light framed her kind face. "Oh, give me a break. She had it coming."

"I'm Marge." The lady extended her hand slightly, but pulled it back when Vicki took no notice. "Don't be too harsh on Dorothy. She's trying to get everything organized. I have a feeling she means well."

Vicki drew up her left leg, caressing her right calf with her toes. "Marge, I can be as harsh as I want as long as I look like this."

Marge shook her head. "You're missing the point."

"Get real. Do you think for one minute Preston would choose you or that loud-mouthed cow over me?"

"Haven't you ever heard the old adage, beauty's only skin deep? A man never chooses a whore for a wife."

"Who're you calling a whore?"

"Why, no one. I'm just relating a fact of life, but if the shoe fits—" Marge held her chin high and left.

"Get real, old woman!" Vicki jumped up and slammed her door. "Being young and beautiful does not make me a whore!" She caught her reflection in the dresser mirror and burst out laughing. "Well, Victoria Truchard, you've already got them going."

CHAPTER THREE

Journal entry—March 1ˢᵗ
What a piece of work. I figured she'd be fun, but I had no idea how much. She'll rub them all raw before this deal is over.

While Vicki finished her beauty nap and Dorothy made the rounds taking notes, the only real cook in the group figured she better see to lunch. Soft steps on the hard Mexican tile didn't pull her from her mission. If whoever had come to help, fine. Otherwise, she didn't have time for an idle conversation. She dug around in a lower cabinet then fished out a large serving bowl.

"Hi, you Audrey?"

She stood straight, set the bowl on the counter, and opened the Miracle Whip. "That'd be me."

"The bossy one with the clipboard told me I should help with lunch."

"Good." Audrey finished spreading a piece of wheat bread. "And you are? Sorry, I'm not very good with names and with meeting so many—"

"Oh, I understand. Charlotte, Charlotte Rushing. Pleased to meet you." Her southern drawl seemed slightly exaggerated, but who could resist being intrigued? The slender woman smiled, stuck out her hand, then pulled it back. "Sorry, silly me. You're busy."

Audrey handed her the knife. "Here. How about you spread, and I'll put on the fixings?"

"Sounds like a plan to me." The Southern Belle crammed the blade into the jar, scraped it against the sides, and pulled out a teetering white glob. She held the knife in midair. "How about I do some mustard ones, too?"

"That would be nice." The glob plopped onto the speckled, soft pink counter. Maybe letting her help wasn't such a good idea after all.

"Oh, I am so sorry. Clumsy me."

"Well, don't be sorry." Audrey smiled to make certain her tone sounded friendly. "Just grab a rag and clean it up." She doubted the belle had prepared many meals. "I love your accent. You from Georgia?"

She shook her head. "North Carolina," then headed for the sink. "Can you believe this beautiful kitchen?"

"It's something else all right. Have you seen the pantry?"

"No, ma'am, I guess I haven't seen much of anything—" Ma'am? Audrey wasn't that much older. This gal might be carrying her southern charm a little too far. "—but I surely do love this kitchen, don't you?" Charlotte swiped once at her mess then threw the soiled dishrag in the sink's direction.

Yes, Audrey definitely loved it, especially the six Tiffany-style stained glass shades that hung over the L-shaped counter. The hues of green, lavender, and blue in the grassy dragonfly pattern were her favorite colors. And the island behind her that separated the serving area from the over-sized stove and sink, a perfect touch.

She turned and rinsed the rag. "I love the whole house from what I've seen, but the kitchen's by far my favorite. It has as many square feet as my entire apartment." She walked over and finished wiping up the woman's mess.

"Sorry, didn't I get it well enough? All I usually do is shrimp and lobster."

Audrey ignored the apology. "According to Preston, this counter's solid granite from right here in Texas."

"Why, imagine that." Charlotte pulled her fingertips over the cool stone. She walked toward the east wall and nodded at the ten-foot, glass-front floor-to-ceiling cabinets. All sorts of collectibles filled them, and arranged across the top, an interesting medley of old hurricane lamps finished them off.

"I just love antiques, don't you? See that pretty oil lamp up there? The one that has the round etched glass globe over the long-necked one? It's got a cast iron base."

"The fifth one over?"

The southern beauty counted with her finger. "Yes, that's it. I think if we could get it down, you could see that that little gold sticker right at the top is the original Scottish label. A lovely piece. I believe it even has all original parts, too. Sure looks like it—the brass details, china knobs. Why, it appears the lamp's hardly been used since it was new over a hundred years ago." She turned back to face Audrey. "I'd place it in the late eighteen hundreds."

Maybe something a little more solid than air filled that pretty head after all. "I'm impressed. How did you know all that?"

"Oh, my Granny loved antiques. Had her own shop. When I was just a tiny bitty thing, she used to drag me all over searching for pieces to keep it full. Did a right smart business out of that little storefront. By the time I turned fourteen, she had me appraising for customers and setting the shop's prices."

"Well, I'm sure Mr. Preston was duly impressed. I'd say you have more than a couple of steps up on the others since he obviously shares your love of old things."

"Maybe, but I'm not sure he knows."

A closer inspection of the first cabinet's contents earned a chorus of ooos and ahs and why,-lookie-here's from the Southern Belle. Remarks made on different items supported her Granny story, too.

Audrey shook her head and continued lunch preparations.

Dorothy swished into the room and flopped in the nearest chair. Her clipboard slammed to the table with a jarring slap. "I've got it all lined out, but we have a lazy little bimbo among us, ladies. The nerve of some people! She races to claim the biggest room then has the audacity to tell me she doesn't 'do domestic'—like she's some kind of princess or something. You know?"

Audrey sliced the last tomato and picked up a purple onion. "You're speaking of the one who came in late aren't you? Vicki, wasn't it? I pegged her from the start."

The woman nodded. "That's the one. And obviously," she made imaginary quotation marks with her fingers, "the *only* one to hear her tell it."

Audrey covered the sliced onions with a patterned dish-towel. "When she drug herself in this morning, I thought 'Now there's a boy-toy if I ever saw one'. The way she headed straight for that room, you've got to figure she must have had the grand tour." She quirked an eyebrow. "Grander tour than I had, anyway, and no telling what else."

"You know, I don't care if she's Preston's personal prostitute. Nothing gives her the right to speak to me the way she did."

"Now, Dorothy." Marge stood in the doorway. "Don't be too hard on her. She was a bit rude to me, too, but we need to be tolerant and kind to one another. I'm sure we're all feeling a little awkward. I know I am." She came in and sat across from the offended woman. "She looked like she had a rough night, and you probably caught her at a bad time."

Audrey laughed. "You've got that right. Told me this morning she'd stayed up until three. She blew the last thousand of her bonus on a fling."

"See?"

Dorothy scooted to the edge of her seat. "Oh, please. Don't be so naïve, you know? That little twit will walk all over us if we let her, and I, for one, do not intend to allow it."

"Whatever you think." Marge rose and straightened her long skirt.

Audrey set the knife in the sink and rinsed the cutting board. "Anyone want to round up everybody? It's almost noon. Sandwiches are ready, and the soup's hot."

"Hey, we're here." Dorothy raised her chin and smoothed her neck. "They all heard Mr. Preston say noon, you know? I sure hope he plans to explain more than he did this morning about what he expects from everyone."

Marge glanced at her, shrugged, then disappeared. Charlotte, now standing before the sixth cabinet, continued to scrutinize the knick-knacks. Audrey grinned. What had she gotten herself into? In the beginning, the whole concept seemed fun, now she wasn't so sure.

What reason under the sun would Preston have to invite so many diverse women to participate in his bizarre game? But then maybe there had been lies on their applications, too. She turned and sighed aloud. "Oh, well."

Marge returned with three women. "Vicki didn't answer when I knocked, but just to remind everyone who's who, Natalie, Holly, and Virginia." She pointed at each lady beside her respectively. "Dorothy, Charlotte, and Audrey—who you can thank for lunch." Marge took a seat at the far table. Wasn't hard to see why Preston had chosen her. She exuded kindness and grace. That lady would be one to keep an eye on.

The kitchen buzzed with the women's exchange of information and a few thank-yous for the lunch preparations.

Audrey filled the tureen at the stove then moved the soup to the serving counter. "Welcome, welcome, but it's no big deal. I love to cook, and I'm in heaven in this kitchen. It's so well designed."

"My wife's dream." The male voice turned all heads, including her own. Preston stood at the far end. "Nancy and I stayed awake many a night discussing all the things she wanted in here."

"And I just love these cabinets and all these wonderful treasures. You really have some exquisite pieces, Mr. Preston. Why, this collection must have taken years." Charlotte returned to the serving area and picked up an empty plate.

Dorothy stepped over to the host and gave him her Miss America smile. "Everything's ready."

Audrey could hardly believe her ears. Like she had anything to do with it. The nerve of some people.

The credit-taker looped her arm through Preston's. "How would you like the tables arranged?"

He patted her hand. "Sorry, but a problem's popped up, and I don't have time for a sit-down lunch today." He politely freed his arm then gestured toward the plate of sandwiches. "Audrey, if you would be so kind as to sack up four of those. Hate to miss the soup. It smells great."

"Maybe you can have a bowl when you come in." She pulled out a drawer and retrieved a box of plastic bags.

He looked impressed. "Found your way fast, girl."

"Not really. That's where I would have put them." She met his gaze and smiled, then stuffed two sandwiches into each bag.

Preston paused at the door on his way out. "We'll have a sit down at six." He spun. "Dorothy, use that long table." He pointed toward the north wall. "The leaves are in the closet on the porch. Seat everyone by age. Me at the head with the oldest on my right, in order, around to the youngest on my left."

"Yes, sir." The organizer seemed thrilled with such explicit instructions. "Anything else?"

He shook his head then hollered back on his way out. "Leave Jorje a place at the other end."

The belle chose a sandwich from the tray then leaned over and covered her mouth. "Do you suppose he's gonna eat four sandwiches for lunch?"

"Maybe he's taking two for Jorje." Audrey smiled sweetly.

"I don't like that wetback of his." Dorothy got in line behind Miss North Carolina. "He's got shifty eyes. You know? Probably carries a pistol in his boot."

Holly—her name was easy to keep straight because her chest resembled Dolly's—took a deep breath then exhaled. "You sure have an imagination. He doesn't have shifty eyes, and how would you know whether or not he's a wetback? I bet he's legal."

"I have to agree with Holly." Marge knitted her brows. "The day I came to interview, Jorje seemed very nice. I'd say he's shy maybe, not shifty."

"Well, I don't care what any of you say. Mexicans are all alike, you know—the whole bunch of them." Dorothy waved off the room and filled herself a plate. "We'll need some bowls."

"That's something I can do." Charlotte sat her plate down and started fanning cabinets.

Audrey opened the right one on the first try. "Here they are, sweetie." She smiled warmly at the blank expression on

Charlotte's face. "The bowls?"

"Oh. Why, yes. Thanks."

The buzz returned as the women fixed their plates and began eating. Audrey got hers last. When finished, she put her dishes in the sink then retired to her room.

She busied herself with a new mystery by Tricia Allen for an hour or so before returning to the kitchen. Only one lady remained. The diminutive dark-skinned woman with a long ponytail stood over the sink, but Audrey couldn't remember her name. The girl wrung out the dishrag and hung it folded across the sink's divider.

"Hello again." She nodded and smiled.

"Hi. Hope you don't mind if I have to ask your name. I'm not as good with remembering as I used to be."

The girl looked up and grinned sheepishly. Her almond eyes shone as black as her hair. Her exotic Polynesian features made you wonder where she was from or what mix she was. "Oh, no prob. I'm Natalie Bastian from Austin. Where're you from?"

"Grew up on a sheep ranch near Meridian, south and west of here, but I've spent my adult life in the big city—Houston. So what do you think of this place so far?"

"It's okay. I mean the house is wonderful and everyone seems nice. It's—well, it's hard for me to get to know new people sometimes, especially women, and there're so many. I can't imagine why Mr. Preston chose me or why I accepted. I think it was something in his eyes I couldn't resist."

"He's handsome enough all right. I'd say don't worry about the other, after a few months with this group, I'm thinking we'll know each other plenty well." Audrey tied an apron around her waist and put two chickens she found in the refrigerator on to boil.

"You cooking dinner, too?"

34

"It isn't a chore, I enjoy it."

"God bless you for that. I was never much good in the kitchen. I can't figure out what I want to do, but I knew I could handle clean up. Sure surprised me when no one else stayed to help, though."

Audrey picked through fruit in an enormous bowl on the counter. "I guess everyone's still feeling their way around."

The pixie excused herself, and Audrey rinsed her selections. She hummed as she cut a salad in the peaceful quiet. A few of the varieties of fruits she couldn't identify, but chopped them, tasted to see if they were good, then added them if they were. Only tossed one that had too many seeds. Topping the creation with whipped cream and nuts, she sat the salad in the refrigerator to chill.

"Audrey?"

Her back was to the door, but how could she miss that accent? "Yes, Charlotte?"

"I just can't seem to find a TV anywhere around here. Have you seen one?"

Audrey squatted in front of the fridge and rummaged through the crisper. Balancing her choices in the apron skirt, she answered without looking around. "No, come to think of it, I don't guess I have. Maybe there aren't any."

"But my stories." She looked as if she might actually shed tears. "Why, I never dreamed I'd have to miss my stories. Erica Kane was fixing to get married again. How will I ever keep up?"

The girl's seriousness tickled Audrey, and she couldn't help but chuckle. "Charlotte, how old are you?"

"Why, thirty-three. Why is it you ask?"

"Oh, seems to me you need to get a life if a silly television show means that much. I never understood a soap's appeal. At least, they're not real life." She stood, spilled the contents of her apron into the sink, then rinsed the vegetables, stopping only long enough to grab two cutting boards. "Want to get me some potatoes from the pantry?" She went back to scrubbing. "I've got chicken and rice, but you know how some men like potatoes with every meal."

"Sure." The semi-airhead slash antique-specialist walked around the corner. "Uh, I'm sorry, but I'm afraid I can't find the pantry."

Audrey laid her head back and closed her eyes. "Do you see the arched door there in front of you?"

"Yes, ma'am."

"There's no reason to call me ma'am, Charlotte. I'm not *that* much older than you. Open the door."

"Well, my gracious, I never. Would you just look at this. Why, I've never laid eyes on such a huge pantry! It's a whole room, isn't it?" Her face popped into a curtained window beside the stove. "Lookie. Here I am. I bet this used to be the back of the house, huh? That fancy door sure doesn't look like it belongs to a pantry, does it? So how many potatoes did you need?"

In spite of Charlotte's help, everything was ready by five forty-five. Dorothy came early and inserted the leaves in the table. She asked everyone's age as the ladies drifted in one by one.

Audrey placed the rolls on the table as the seated women shifted yet again. She looked around and suggested someone go for Vicki. No one moved. "Charlotte, would you mind reminding her that Mr. Preston wants us for supper at six?"

"Well, actually, I'd really like to avoid that one as much as possible. I surely don't mean to be disagreeable, but—"

"Oh, for goodness sakes. I'll go tell her. Why make a big fuss over nothing?"

Dorothy laughed. "You hit the nail on the head, Marge.

That bimbo's nothing to fuss over, that's for certain, don't you know?"

"Who are you calling a bimbo?" Dressed in a slinky, sequined cocktail dress, Vicki made her entrance in full make-up with her frosted hair piled in ringlets. How she spent the day since lunch was no secret. She glared at the name-caller.

Dorothy didn't look away. "You know, I imagine you've probably been called worse."

Audrey slipped between the cat and kitty. "That's enough, ladies. I worked too hard on this meal for you two to ruin it. Now, sit down and behave."

"Vicki, how old are you, dear?" Marge touched her arm.

"Twenty-seven."

"The youngest. You'll sit on the end next to Natalie." The Polynesian princess waved her fingers. "Right there, dear." Marge pointed to the empty chair, sat in the one directly across, then turned to her right and smiled. "I thought I'd be the oldest. Aren't these youngsters something?"

"Definitely." Virginia looked around the table. "But don't let their youth intimidate you. Not a one of them has skin any prettier than yours."

"Aren't you sweet. I've been a Mary Kay customer since my twenties, so will give credit where credit's due."

Audrey took her seat across from Charlotte and on the other side of Virginia. "Glad to see you beside me since we haven't got to visit much." She turned to her right. "You, too, Dorothy. Give us a chance to know each other better." She offered her hand to both, squeezed gently, smiling at Holly on the other corner. "Have y'all gotten all settled in?"

Charlotte nodded. "I'm all unpacked. I got the upstairs room on the right with the view of the back yard. I think they're bigger than the ones downstairs."

Virginia scooted her chair toward the table. "Pretty much.

I'm just dying to hear from the man, aren't you? This whole deal is so odd."

Big Boobs leaned forward. "Well, I sure am. I mean, he's such a hunk!"

The wait wasn't long. On the clock's sixth gong, Preston and Jorje walked into the suddenly silent kitchen. Taking his seat at the head of the table, he fluffed his napkin and spread it across his lap. He took a sip of water then cleared his throat.

"Anyone care to pray before we eat?"

"Thank you, Mr. Preston. I certainly would." Marge bowed her head.

Audrey scanned the table during the prayer. When she reached Preston, she realized he had been doing the same. Their eyes locked. Oh, no, you don't, Mr. Winston Grant Preston. I've played that game before. She stared for a minute then tried to swallow to quell a rising rumble, but couldn't come up with enough spit. She finally bowed in desperation.

"—we give thanks. Amen."

"Thank you, Marge." He picked up the steamed potatoes, helped himself to a large portion, then passed the bowl to his right. "My wife was a praying woman."

Other than the sounds of knives and forks clinking against the eclectic dinnerware or an occasional request to pass something, the ten diners ate in a relative hush. Audrey wondered if Preston noticed the dirty looks Dorothy kept shooting in Vicki's direction but decided he most likely didn't. His obvious gusto for eating kept his attention pretty well focused.

Finally, he pushed his plate away. "Wonderful meal, Audrey! You must be a believer in that old adage about the way to a man's heart." He leaned back in his chair.

"Thank you." She gave him a slight nod and tried not to

smile too big. She felt, rather than saw, the other women exchange glances. "There's pie and coffee when you're ready."

"Maybe later." He smiled while Dorothy scraped the casserole dish. "Has everyone settled in okay? Found the linen closet? Everything you need?" He paused. Each lady nodded or voiced approval of the accommodations. "Good."

He sat forward and rubbed his hands together. "The way I've decided to work this deal is to send one of you home at the end of each month."

Dorothy looked up surprised. "But you didn't say anything about that when you hired me."

"Didn't decide until today, but I also said you could leave anytime. You want to go now?"

"No, of course not. I don't want to leave."

"Good." He leaned back in his chair again. "So. Anybody have any questions?"

A hand shot into the air. Audrey smiled knowing what the question would be. "Are there any televisions in the house? I couldn't find one this afternoon."

"Afraid not. I hate the things."

Charlotte's face showed disappointment, but she said no more.

"Mr. Preston?" Dorothy nodded in Vicki's direction. "What are you going to do about the slackers?" Poor lady, doesn't she realize she's not making points. Surely she wanted to be the next Mrs. Preston as much as anyone, but couldn't she see the error of her way?

"You think someone's not doing their part?"

"Won't call names, but someone in your employ doesn't seem too willing to pull her weight."

"Dorothy, do you remember what I hired you to do?"

She shifted her eyes seemingly looking for advocates then back to Preston. "Be myself?"

39

"That's right. And I told everyone the same thing. So far, I have no complaints."

Audrey covered a snicker by clearing her throat. She leaned forward and whispered, "And I thought this wasn't going to be any fun!"

"I'm saying." Holly leaned across the table toward Dorothy. "Can you put me down to cook dinner tomorrow?"

CHAPTER FOUR

Journal entry—March 2ⁿᵈ
*Such passion. Looks like I was right, but time will tell. I
have been wrong before—though not very often.*

The bliss of fresh-brewed coffee floated on the early morning
air. Marge rested deep in Delta sleep, but the inviting smell
wooed her to consciousness. She opened her eyes. At first, the
unfamiliar room startled her then brought a smile to her face.
Her bedside clock read four forty-five. She rolled out of the
antebellum four-poster, stepped into her slippers, grabbed her
robe, and followed her nose toward the aromatic brew.

Once she cleared the hall, a single light shadowed Preston's unmistakable silhouette on the screened back porch.
The French doors stood open. She froze halfway to the
kitchen.

"Good morning, Marge. Sleep well?" He rose and passed
her with a determined stride.

"Yes, thank you." Her feet refused to carry her anywhere,
so she stood there somewhat uncomfortable, though she
couldn't say why. After a moment, she slowly followed him
into the kitchen. He refilled his own mug and poured a
second. She accepted his offering. "Uh, I smelled the—I
didn't expect you."

He led her back out onto the porch and moved a wicker

chair opposite the one he had been sitting in. "I don't sleep much any more."

She sat on the edge of the chair and blew the coffee. With her free hand, she clutched her robe closed though the pre-dawn air wasn't cold. "Neither do I, usually, but I slept much better last night than I anticipated, being in a strange bed and all."

"Glad you were comfortable." He propped his feet on the wicker coffee table and fell silent as he sipped his coffee.

While the silence reigned, Marge didn't know what to do, so she enjoyed the stillness and stared out into the darkness. After a few minutes that seemed more like forty, she stood. "Maybe I'll go read for awhile."

He touched her arm and raised his cup. "Stay out here. I'll go get us some more."

"No, let me."

"Already on the way. You sit." She eased back into her chair while he rose to fetch the coffeepot. He topped off their mugs. "This is the best time of the day."

She blew gently on the hot liquid. "Actually, I guess it's more like the middle of the night, but I know what you mean. I love it, too."

He chuckled on his way back to the kitchen. "In the oil patch, it's already the middle of the morning."

She waited until he returned. "Tell me Mr.—" She paused. "What do you want us to call you, anyway?"

He squinted one eye, staring at her with the other. "On the bayou, everyone has a basket name." He opened his eyes wide. "A secret name spoken only at special times because it wields tremendous power." He leaned in. "Mine's Buck."

She grinned. "Are you making this up?"

"No. Buck's my basket name." He held up both hands, palms out. "An old black man gave it to me when I was ten."

"So you want us to call you Buck?"

He shook his head. "Not everyone." He pointed to her. "But you can use it if we're alone and the sun isn't up."

Why would he be telling her such a yarn? She leaned forward. "Now you are pulling my leg. I always was too gullible."

He frowned. "No. It's true, and I just gave you power over me."

She leaned back and drank a swallow. The seriousness of his tone knocked her off balance. Unsure how to respond, she looked around, wanted to go to her room and think, but like a child in a candy store, found it difficult to leave. From the start, this man's myriad complexities lured her. She hid behind her cup, gathering her wits.

"So," she finally asked, "what does everyone call you when the sun's up?"

He shrugged. "When I was a kid, an old maid aunt called me Dub. I always liked that, but it didn't stick."

"I like it, too." She nodded. "Dub it is then."

"But don't tell anyone. Just start using it."

His easy manner amazed Marge. A few minutes after false dawn, a rooster's crow split the calm. Preston jumped to his feet, grabbed her hand, and pulled her out the screen door to the backyard. The eastern horizon blazed with the beginnings of a new day.

He guided her to a rattan rocker. "Sit here and watch the sun come up. I'll get us more coffee." This time he took her cup.

The rooster crowed again. Why was Preston acting like this? He couldn't be seriously interested in her with all those beautiful younger women around. A trickle of water fell over a flat boulder into a small pond that sheltered the south end of the flagstone patio.

He reappeared.

Marge took the steaming coffee and cocked her head slightly. "Do you know what you are? I've got it figured out."

"What?"

Marge let the thought ferment a moment. "You're just a big kid, and we ladies are your new toys."

He slapped his chest and threw his head back. "Oh, to suffer the slings and arrows of words unjustly spoken. Thou dost truly wound me, Fair Lady."

She bit her lip, but couldn't stop her eyes from laughing. "And where, pray tell, did that come from?"

"Wasn't it a line from MacBeth?"

Who was he trying to fool now? "I hardly think so."

"You sure? Sounded pretty good to me."

"Back to what I was saying. This is all a big joke to you. A game, isn't it?"

He stared off in the direction of the rising sun. "No, Marge. I want a wife, even more than before now that the house is full of beautiful women."

Something was wrong. He didn't act like a man hunting a wife.

"Hey, what're you two doing out here?"

"Good morning, Audrey." Preston lifted his mug. "Grab a cup and help us watch the sun come up. Looks like another glorious day."

She soon returned carrying her own steaming mug and sat next to him.

Marge smiled. "It is beautiful, isn't it? Did that delicious smell of coffee wake you, too?" She couldn't remember the last time she and a man had seen a sunrise together, and even the intrusion of the pretty cook couldn't spoil the moment. It lightened her heart. For a moment she let herself fantasize about a life with Dub. She raised an eyebrow. Or should she say Buck?

44

"Well, enough lounging around for me." Preston stood. "If you'll excuse me, ladies. I have an orchard to tend."

Marge touched his arm. "Speaking of the orchard, where are those apple trees? I meant to ask."

"You passed them when you came in."

She cocked her head. "I did? I don't remember seeing them."

The interloper stretched and yawned. "Neither do I, come to think of it."

"On the trellises, ladies." He handed his mug to the blonde. "See you at lunch."

"Don't you want breakfast?" Audrey stood beside him, barely reaching his shoulder. She tilted her head back and looked into his eyes. Had a spark passed between them? Marge had to admit, Audrey would be a good choice. They made a striking couple.

"No, thanks." He walked toward the house. "Only eat lunch and supper."

"Have a good day, Dub."

"What did you call him?"

Marge faced her rival and put on her best smile of perceived innocence. "Didn't I call him Mr. Preston?"

"No. Sounded like Dub, and he nodded his head." Audrey smiled and with much exaggeration, slowly moved her head up and down. "I see, I see. And exactly what have y'all been up to this morning?"

Marge stood. "Coffee and the start of a new day." She stuck her free hand in her robe pocket and strolled to her room. She almost pulled a Vicki and snuggled back into bed, but decided more sleep would only keep her awake that night and make it harder to get up early.

The morning slipped by. She read, chatted with a few of the women, and daydreamed. Much to her regret, Jorje fetched lunch. Hoping maybe he'd change his mind and come in, she lingered in the kitchen. After her third lapse into fantasy land, her practical side erupted. "Well, this is ridiculous." Her words, intended as thoughts, echoed around the kitchen.

Charlotte looked up from scrubbing potatoes. "What's ridiculous?"

"What he's doing to us."

Big-chested Holly entered from the hall carrying the vacuum. "What who's doing to us?" She crossed the kitchen and put it away in the pantry.

Audrey, who had been thumbing through one of Preston's many cookbooks, looked up. "Yes, please, do tell."

Marge spread her hands. "Can't you all see?" She paused, searching each face. "He's making us all fall in love, not so much with him, but his house, his money, and the implied promise that one of us will win his wedding lottery."

Holly laughed. "Hey, I swallowed his bait from the get-go. Just let him give my line one little jerk, and watch me gladly slip into his lap and jump around. I'd love to be his fish out of water." The other ladies laughed but not Marge.

She sighed and shook her head. "You're missing the point. Didn't you hear what he said? He's going to send one of us home each month. In no time, if we don't guard against it, those left will be at each other's throats."

Audrey leaned back, fingered the book for a second, then looked at Marge. "You've got a point. I'll have to admit to being a little miffed this morning."

Charlotte leaned over the counter. "What happened this morning?"

"Nothing." Marge scanned their faces. "But don't you see? This is only the second day, and he's already got us worried, suspicious, and jealous of one another."

"Well, just what do you suppose we're going to do?" Holly pulled out a chair next to Marge.

At the thought of leaving, a lead weight fell down Marge's throat and sunk to the pit of her stomach. "I don't know. Maybe I'm wrong, but—"

Charlotte dried her hands on a towel then twirled it so hard, Marge felt the breeze on her cheek. "Will someone tell me what happened this morning?"

Marge glanced at her. "Preston and I had coffee on the porch this morning. That's all. Nothing else happened."

Holly touched Marge's arm and glared at Charlotte. "You stopped at 'but' before you were so rudely interrupted. Finish what you meant to say."

"Well, it's just that I've been fantasizing all day about a life in this house. I mean, just the linen closet. Everything in there felt like two hundred thread count, and I don't know what he's been using for softener, but when I was making my bed, I thought I might faint from the bliss of that fresh smell."

As an exotic fragrance of expensive perfume wafted into the kitchen, Marge looked over her shoulder. Vicki stood in the doorway. "Any woman who wouldn't love this house is a fool, but what about the man? How do you feel about Preston?"

"I can't answer that fairly yet. I hardly know him."

"Well, I do, and I can tell you he's not who he appears to be." Vicki sauntered to the coffeepot and poured herself a cup. "Didn't even go to college. Doesn't that surprise you? Spent most of his life in the oil patch." She sipped the thick brew left in the pot since morning, but that's how she probably drank it most of the time. "You're trying to make him out to be some kind of Harvard psychology major, but he's just an old roughneck with money."

Charlotte spoke up. "And, if I may ask, how is it that you know him so well?"

"Research. The Dallas Public Library isn't five stories because it's filled with fiction. Someone with the wealth of Winston Grant Preston can't keep his name out of the papers." She sat her cup down and headed out. "Just don't ever make the mistake of—" She paused. "Never mind."

"Wait. Mistake of what?" Holly jumped to her feet and whirled Vicki around. "You can't say something like that then leave with a 'never mind'."

The beauty queen looked at her arm then at Holly. "You're the soap freak?"

Holly released her and nodded toward the table. "No. I mean, I did watch them, but that would be Miss Charlotte there."

The belle looked offended. "Why, I don't see any reason at all to get nasty. What's wrong with a soap opera?"

Vicki's face softened. "I was going to say don't make the mistake of calling him Winnie." She strolled out, calling over her shoulder. "He killed a man once for it."

For several minutes, silence rang in Marge's ears. Audrey's chair scooted across the flagstone floor and exploded the quiet as she stood and returned to her cooking. The other women drifted out, and Marge eventually followed when the shock wore off.

She paced her room and tried to convince herself that Vicki couldn't be telling the truth. Even if she didn't know him that well, surely Dub wouldn't kill a man just for calling him a name. But if he did—

She retrieved her suitcase from under the bed and started packing, changed her mind, unpacked it and put everything back. She opened her book to read but never got through the first paragraph. She pulled her bag out again, but when she heard Charlotte's supper call, stuffed it half-packed back under the bed. Two more times around the room and a quick check of her reflection in the bathroom mirror convinced her to stay at least another day. Straightening her blouse, she turned and marched to the kitchen.

Already in their chairs, everyone turned when Marge walked in. Preston stood and smiled, bowing slightly at the waist.

"Dub, did you kill a man for calling you a name?"

The smile disappeared. Preston sunk to his chair, leaned back, and folded his arms across his chest. "I don't know who you've been talking to, but someone sure didn't tell you the whole story."

"Well? Did you or didn't you?"

"Sit down, Marge. Let's eat, then I'll tell you all about it."

CHAPTER FIVE

Journal entry—March 2nd
After so many years, I can still feel my fist crushing his jaw.
Of all the things I've done, I wish I could take that back the
most.

Preston laid down his fork and studied his empty plate. He
shouldn't tell them anything; they didn't need to know, but an
eerie silence prevailed through dinner—unusual when eating
with so many women. When he looked up, eight pairs of eyes
bored into him. Yeah, guess they needed to know all right,
unless he wanted them all to leave, and he didn't.

"I was twenty-three, and two days back from my first trip
off shore." He paused and peered into the past; it had been
forever since he'd thought about that night. In half a heart-
beat, he was that hotheaded roughneck out looking for a good
time.

"I pushed past the drugstore cowboy watching the door to
the Ol' Top Rail. 'Hey, boy.' The man grabbed my arm. 'Let
me see it.' Before my tongue could get me in trouble, my right
hand whipped out my driver's license. He looked at the piece
of paper. 'What's your middle name?' I says, 'Grant, why?'

"The man shrugged. 'You're big enough, but you don't
look old enough.' I grabbed my license and stepped into the
dimly lit honky-tonk. For sixteen ear-splitting bars of the

way-too-loud western swing some local bunch of wannabes were throwing out as music, I let my eyes adjust to the lack of light. Shame my ears couldn't do likewise, but if you wanted to rub bellies with the ladies, you had to suffer.

"A round of long-necks and three trips around the well-worn hardwood bought me an invite to sit at the table with a trio of not-so-young cowgirls. Mercifully, the band stopped their off-key yodeling and sick cat torturing."

Preston rolled his neck, then rubbed his ears. "Thinking about it still hurts. Seems to me too many bands think loud and good are one and the same." He looked again into the past.

"Anyway, the lady on my right hip scooted her chair closer and winked. 'How about a real drink?' She had a husky voice. 'Sure thing, ma'am. What's your poison?' She cuddled my shoulder. 'Old Scotch and big, well-mannered men.' I stood, but she grabbed my forearm. 'Make it a double.'

"After that one, another double, then one last real slow trip around the dance floor, I figured I'd found that night's bedmate. For the next hour while the other two ladies danced, I plied her with more Scotch and sweet words. Just as we'd about talked ourselves into going to my hotel, someone stormed up to the table, grabbed my shoulder, and pulled me around. 'Take a hike, Buster.'

"I found center and jumped to my feet. A guy a good foot shorter than me stood with his hands on his hips glaring. I stuck out my hand. 'Winston Preston, don't believe I know you.' Shorty nodded toward the lady. 'That's my wife.' 'That so?' 'Yeah, now beat it.' I looked over my shoulder. 'He telling the truth?' She shrugged. 'He's only wishing. I left the bum on account of I don't like getting beat up.' I faced the intruder. 'She's with me tonight.'

"The smaller man shook his head. 'Take a hike, Winnie,

or you're gonna be sorry.' 'Don't—' Shorty pulled out a knife and swiped at me. I jerked back then countered with an uppercut to his chin. The guy crumpled to the floor."

Preston stopped his narrative and searched the eight ladies' faces. He detected no condemnation or disbelief. Marge's color had softened, almost returned to it's normal shade.

"Anyway, that's what happened."

Vicki nodded in agreement. She studied her sculptured nails for a second, before looking squarely at the older man. "Mr. Preston, I'm the one who told 'em that you killed a guy for calling you Winnie." She let one side of her mouth creep up, hoping his stern expression would tender and encourage her to finish the smile, but the muscles in his jaw flexed. Did she catch a twinkle in his eyes?

She evoked the memory of when her only childhood pet, an orange tabby, had died in her arms then squeezed a tear out to trickle from the corner of her eye. "I'm sorry, Mr. Preston, really. I shouldn't have shot my mouth off." She leaned back and crossed her legs. Her heart boomed in her ears. "I know I have a problem sometimes about saying things I shouldn't."

She glanced at Marge. "It was wrong to make you out to be some kind of murderer. I should háve explained that the other guy cut you first, and that you only hit him once."

Marge put a hand on top of his. "You killed that man with one blow?"

Preston nodded.

Vicki looked down the table. Everyone seemed to hang on her words. "The grand jury no-billed him, and that was the end of it. Right, Mr. Preston?"

He tossed his head back and stretched his chin. "Except for the dreams."

She laid her hand on his arm. "You're not going to send me home, are you?"

He scanned the women, then nodded once to the far end of the table. "*Amigo,* what do you think?"

She ducked her head while Jorje rattled something in Spanish.

"And you ladies?"

Several spoke at once, but Dorothy continued, so the others relinquished the floor. "I think a week of cooking and kitchen detail should teach her a lesson in decorum."

Vicki glared at the woman then turned back to Preston, pleading internally. Please, not that. Anything but cooking. She gritted her mind, willing him to say no.

"Dorothy thinks kitchen duty's appropriate. Any other ideas?"

Marge took a deep breath then sighed. "Well, she said she was sorry. Since I've made a mistake or two of my own, I say forgive her. To my mind, repentance is enough."

"The lady leans toward grace." He nodded in Marge's direction. "Anyone else?" No one said anything. He scooted his chair away from the table. "Well, I like Jorje's idea. Vicki, if you want to stay in my employ, I want you to have a fresh pot of coffee ready for me when I get up every day this week."

Vicki's stomach relaxed, and the lump in her throat disappeared. She put a thumb up and smiled. "You've got it. No problem! Coffee actually happens to be one of my specialties." She caught Marge's eye and mouthed thank you. The older woman acknowledged with a single nod, but she had a look of having lost her best friend. Maybe she figured she'd just lost a rich husband by being too gracious to the competition.

Preston patted Vicki's shoulder. "Good."

"Mr. Preston, may I have a word in private with you?" Holly asked.

"Sure." He ushered the woman out of the room toward his office.

Vicki grabbed her plate and an empty serving bowl. She scraped the plate's contents into the pile of scraps and flipped on the hot water. She squirted a generous portion of liquid soap into the filling sink while Audrey carried the scraps outside for the cats.

Dorothy put her plate on the counter. "Why, Vicki, you're just full of surprises tonight, aren't you? I thought you didn't do domestic."

Vicki ignored the loudmouth, handed a wet plate to Marge, and regulated the water.

"Hey! I'm talking to you."

Vicki spun. "And I'm ignoring you!" She flicked soapsuds at the older woman just as Audrey came in the side door. "Get a life, freak." Vicki smiled when Dorothy's cheeks flushed red.

Chub wiped the suds from her chin. With one fist on her hip, she fumed, breathing loudly. "Why, you—you—little tramp." She whirled and marched out of the room.

"Whatever." Vicki laughed then returned to the dishes.

Audrey set the empty plate next to Vicki. "I must admit, I didn't want him to send you home."

"Yeah? Why not?"

"Without you here, this place wouldn't be half as much fun."

She looked at Audrey. "So you here just for the fun of it?"

"Well, that's definitely part of the reason I accepted. Guess I was looking for fun. Maybe to add some spice to my life." She swished her fingers in the soapy water, reached around Vicki, and wiped them on Marge's dish towel. "I was stuck in a boring job, working with a bunch of boring people. It had been months," she paused, "actually years, since I'd met anyone like Dub."

"Jorje?"

Audrey jumped at the sound of Preston's voice. She turned in unison with Vicki. The dark man sprang to his boss' side then nodded as Preston whispered into his ear.

He looked toward Vicki, grinned, and walked toward the door. "See you in the morning. Say four-thirty?" Jorje left through the side door.

"Did he say four-thirty?"

Audrey raised both eyebrows. "This morning Marge got up at four forty-five, and he had already made the coffee."

"That's true, I'm afraid."

Vicki frowned, pouted out her bottom lip, and faked a cry. "And I thought he was letting me off light. A whole week! Do either of you have an alarm clock?"

"I do," Marge said. "And you're welcomed to it. I'll get it for you when we're through here."

After drying the last dish, Marge handed her the towel. Vicki dried her hands then followed the older woman to her room. Pulling her suitcase from under the four poster, Marge rummaged through the half-packed Pullman until she came out with an old wind-up clock.

"You're not all unpacked yet?"

"I've been unpacked a couple of times." She gave Vicki a look of slight reprimand. "Just wasn't certain I wanted to stay under the same roof with a murderer."

"Sorry. I really am." While she checked her wristwatch and fiddled to set the clock, Vicki studied the room. "Preston's wife sure did a great job decorating. Don't you think?"

Her advocate extended it toward her. Two silver bells topped the old relic. "She must have been a lovely woman."

Vicki took hold, but Marge didn't release it. Instead she covered Vicki's hand with her other one. "It took a lot of courage for you to admit what you had done."

Vicki laughed. "Well, you sure shocked the crap out of me the way you barged into that room. I'll have to watch what I say a little more carefully around you."

The woman laughed with her, released the clock, and pulled her close into a hug. The gesture startled Vicki. She couldn't remember the last time a woman had hugged her. It made her uncomfortable, and she responded stiffer than intended. It warmed her insides, though, and misted her eyes.

"Four a.m. comes awful early." Marge rubbed her eyes looking like she might start crying herself. She led her toward the door with a hand on Vicki's shoulder. "Better try and get some sleep, honey. I'll see you in the morning."

"Thanks for the clock."

"You're welcome. Good night, dear." Marge closed her door and left Vicki standing in the hall.

She meandered back to the kitchen and peeked in. Holly and Audrey were laughing over a card game. Everyone else had gone. Vicki poured herself a half of a glass of milk and sauntered to their table. She looked from one to the other then shrugged.

"You tell me we're not in competition. I heard Preston say we weren't the same as everyone, but only one of us will be walking beside him to the altar."

"Oh, I figure he's already made up his mind." Audrey played her last card. "I think he's known who he wanted from the start."

Vicki made herself keep a straight face as Audrey continued.

"He's just going through the motions now, having a little fun. Bet he gets a kick out of seein' how we all interact."

"You really think so?" Holly shuffled and reshuffled. "I haven't gotten that impression at all."

Vicki gulped the last swallow of milk. "Well, who is it you think he's already picked?"

"As if you didn't know."

"No, really."

Bottle Blonde grimaced. Big Boobs returned the deck to its box then stretched. "Well, you girls can stay up all night discussing who's going to be the next Mrs. Preston, but I'm going to bed." She rose and started out the door.

"Myself." Vicki rinsed her glass and followed on Holly's heels. "I've stayed up until four-thirty before, but I don't ever remember getting up that early." She laughed at her humor even while she remembered the morning at the Hyatt. Could that have possibly only been two days ago? She rolled her head around, and her neck popped several times. "Night, y'all."

She closed the door then dive bombed her bed. "Yes! I knew it! W.G. decided the minute he met me. Woo hoo, money, money, money! I'll never have to worry about it again."

CHAPTER SIX

Journal entry—March 3rd
I never expected it of her. How'd I ever get by when I didn't have rabbits in my life.

The two men retreated to the office. While the *hombre* melted into the wingback that guarded the massive oak desk, his boss contemplated the situation. Preston loved having the ladies around, but how in the world could he decide on whom to send home first—or second for that matter?

He nodded toward the fridge. "How about a cold one, *amigo?*"

Jorje shook his head. "Nope."

"Why not?"

"You're out of limes."

"So? We can drink a beer without limes."

"No limes, no beer. It's un-Mexican."

"Something else maybe?"

"What do you want?"

"Well, I wanted a beer, but—"

"If you're going to whine about it," the man stood, "I'll get you a beer, but you will drink alone."

Preston smiled just so his friend wouldn't get the total last word, then pulled out his journal. Only the second day, and he already had half a page or more on each of the women, except Virginia. So far she'd done nothing worthy of notation, but could that woman move.

The Mexican plopped back into the chair in front of the grand desk. He set the beer down just out of Preston's reach. "What'd the gal with the big knockers want with you?"

"Well, first of all, when I hired her, they weren't that big. Can't believe she had a boob job. Probably spent my money on it, too. Anyway—" Preston looked at him, then glanced at the bottle, but didn't reach. "She could be your Missie Boss someday. I'd not be referring to her that way if I was a hired hand like some people I know."

"*Si, señor,* a thousand pardons. *Que lastima.*" Jorje grinned. "The possible future Mrs. Preston, huh? What'd she want?"

"If you must know, she's concerned about Virginia."

"Who?"

Preston let the shapely brunette walk across the windows of his soul then smiled. "The tall, graceful one."

Jorje nodded. *"Si, señor. Muy bueno."*

"I know. They all are."

"Not all." His face puckered. "Not the one called Dorothy. You sick that day or something?"

"She's good looking."

"Maybe once. But—"

Preston waved him off. "Beat it. This is my deal, not yours. And you're going to get yourself in trouble if you don't quit insulting the ladies."

He stood. *"Bueno, pero* don't cry to me if you pick wrong."

This time Preston let his friend have the last word without even a grin. He wanted to get the day's events sorted and recorded. This deal promised to be tougher than he thought, but a lot more fun, too.

★ ★ ★ ★ ★

Exactly fifty-six steps northeast, Vicki also sorted and mentally recorded the day's events. She replayed the evening's conversations while waiting for sleep. Audrey's words warmed her heart, but the sadness in Marge puzzled her. What little she knew of the older woman, she didn't seem moody or prone to depression. Maybe she just regretted her accusing outburst.

In the rhythm of the old timepiece, Vicki allowed the day to settle. Snatches of conversations and sly looks played and replayed, first adding depth and texture then full-blown Technicolor to her remembrances. Sometime between the tenth and eleventh rewind, and in spite of the clock's loud metallic ticking, sleep overtook her.

Thoughts of the other women fled, leaving only the man. She dreamed of a life with him, or more precisely, his money.

Before she was ready, the ancient striker beat against the little silver bells. How rude! It couldn't have been more than a few minutes since she drifted off to sleep. She stumbled out of bed, wrapped her robe around herself, and found her fluffy rabbit house shoes.

The sight of them brought a smile and a tug at her heart. They had been the last gift from her mother. The loneliness of having no living relative threatened her again. She looked up and stared at the bed, wondering what woke her and why. "Oh, yeah. Coffee." She gathered herself and forced the bunny shoes down the hall toward the dark kitchen.

Feeling along the wall, she found the switch that lit the kitchen area, then fanned six cabinet doors before finding the one that housed the coffee. "Couldn't've asked where everything was last night and made anything easy on yourself, now, could you?" She eased around, pulling out drawers and muttering to herself. "Where are those blasted filters?"

A man-sized shadow caught her eye. Her heart leapt to her throat. She squealed as the coffee can fell to the floor with a loud clang, bounced twice, then settled on the flagstone with a little metallic ting.

"Easy, darling. It's just me." He rose from the table in the far corner.

"What are you doing hiding over there in the dark like that?" She retrieved the rolling can. "You scared the fool out of me."

"Sorry. Just waiting on my coffee. Wanted to see how you look first thing in the morning, too."

"What time is it? I thought you said—" She paused and bit her lip. "Well, what do you think?" She twisted her hips out, throwing one hand back and the other high in the air. With her wrists bent, she curtsied Betty Boop style.

He chuckled. His laugh was easy and genuine. "Love the shoes. Takes a special kind of woman to wear rabbits."

She laughed then busied herself with the coffee. Her mind raced. Oh, she knew well enough how to get a man into bed, but had no clues for moving one to the altar. She was twelve again, trying to entice the older boys to notice her, but intuition convinced her such tactics wouldn't work with this big guy.

As soon as the pot looked half full, she scabbed a mug for him. "Cream or sugar?"

"Black."

She filled two cups and sat one next to him. "What'cha thinking?" She used her little girl voice.

"Just now, about the orchard, planning my day." He sipped the hot brew. "Not bad."

She turned her face sideways, holding her chin up. "So you weren't admiring how radiant I look in the middle of the night?" She stuck out her bottom lip in an exaggerated pout.

"I admit you look pretty good, even for the middle of—" He tilted his head down a notch and looked from beneath heavy eyebrows. "—the morning, but you could say I'm a bit preoccupied. Got a problem with my trees."

She blew on her own coffee before sipping, then for the next hour, encouraged him to talk about his orchard. Each time he finished a thought, she asked another question. She hung on his words, even found herself laughing at his dry humor.

Sometime between the first and second pot of caffeine, an unfamiliar emotion surged through her. Strong and pure, something she'd always thought herself incapable of.

There had been no interruptions nor any change in the kitchen's illumination, but unaccountably, he shone in a different light. Dollar signs didn't sparkle from his eyes like before. Instead, the depth and kindness she saw impressed her.

She held up both hands, palms toward him. "Stop, you've got to stop." She hugged herself, tears wet her cheeks. "I can't believe—" She sniffed. "Sorry, I have to go."

"What? Why? What's the matter?"

"Never mind." She jumped up, ran to her room, then threw herself across her bed.

A light tapping pulled Marge from her book. She wrapped her robe tight, slipped into her house shoes, and hurried to the door.

"Yes?"

"Open up. It's me."

She cracked it. Preston's rugged features, silhouetted in the dim hall light, greeted her. His eyes belied the slight smile on his lips.

"Sorry to disturb you, but I saw the light under your door.

Would you do me a huge favor?"

"Certainly, if I can."

"It's Vicki." He looked worried. "Don't know what I did. We were drinking coffee and having a nice chat, then she jumped up and ran to her room." He looked down the hall. "Would you check on her? Please."

She patted his chest. "Sure, Dub. I'll be happy to." Oh, she should've called him Buck! They were alone and the sun wasn't up, but she'd missed the opportunity.

He seemed to want to say more but turned and disappeared around the corner. Marge padded down the hall to the last room on the right. She knocked lightly twice. Hearing no answer, she eased the door open a crack. Vicki lay across her bed with her face buried in her pillow.

"You okay?"

She didn't respond.

Marge stepped in. "Vicki, dear, Dub asked me to look in. Are you okay?" She stepped toward the bed. "Because I have to say you don't seem like you are."

"Yes. I am. Really." She rolled over and wiped her cheeks. "He did? He asked you to check on me?"

"Yes, just now."

She sat up then patted the bed next to her. "I hate him."

Marge sat next to the younger woman, her interest peaked past curiosity. "Oh, my goodness. What happened?"

Vicki shook her head, grabbed a tissue off the bedside table, and daubed her eyes. "I—It's—" Vicki swung around and faced Marge. She looked so vulnerable, not at all like the seductive vamp at dinner the night before. "It's just never happened to me. Never in my whole life have I felt about a man the way I felt about Dub this morning." She sniffed, her bottom lip quivered, then tears filled her eyes. "What if he doesn't pick me?"

The question hung in the still morning air for a second, then she closed her eyes as tiny rivulets streamed down her face. Marge didn't know what else to do, so she wrapped her arms around Vicki, and stroked the back of her head.

Indeed, what if?

Vicki snuggled into the caresses at first then jumped to her feet. "This can't be happening." Her faced contorted. "I am not falling in love with a man old enough to be my father."

"Well, don't be too hard on yourself, sweetheart. I think he's an easy man to love."

Vicki clapped her hands once then threw a nod at Marge. "You're right. He is easy to love, kinda like an old dog or a favorite uncle, not that I ever had either, but that's the deal. It's got to be. I just like him a lot. I'm not falling in love with him, right?"

"Sounds good to me." Marge heard herself, but her heart wasn't in the response. Mixed emotions clouded her reason. She didn't want the beautiful young woman to be in love with Dub. The what-if-he-doesn't-pick-me question had taken its turn and plagued her as well, and the more she contemplated it, the more she hated this game.

Vicki's bottom lip quivered. "I'm lying, and the worst of it is, I'm lying to myself. I had a cat once that I loved, but what I felt this morning couldn't be compared. It wasn't anything like that." She grabbed more tissues then flung herself back across the bed.

Marge reached out then drew back and folded her hands into her lap. How had she gotten herself into this mess? But any thoughts of her leaving could no longer be tolerated. She admired this man's truthfulness, his integrity.

He could have gone to Vicki's room instead of asking her to, he could have taken advantage of her. And he didn't have to explain about killing that man, but chose to be open and forthcoming—a wonderful and rare quality in these days and times.

She gently patted Vicki's shoulder then stood. A sigh escaped as she closed the girl's door. She looked up hoping to see him there. She tiptoed to the end of the hall then peeked around the corner wishing he would be waiting for her—to tell him what was wrong with Vicki, of course.

Oh, who was she kidding? Certainly not herself. She wanted him to be there for another chance to look into his eyes, speak with him. She wanted to be the next Mrs. Winston Preston just as badly as the girl crying down the hall.

CHAPTER SEVEN

Journal entry—March 30th
It surprised me how much I missed her. Longest afternoon
I've spent since I couldn't tell you when.

Preston knew nothing of Vicki or Marge's growing affections. The older woman passed the younger's outburst off as female troubles when he inquired later in the day as to her well-being. Not ignorant of feminine mood swings, he let it go, but still pondered why she had left so abruptly.

The days melded into a week then threatened to end the first full month, and his concern over who would be the first sent home and how that process might take place captured the majority of his thoughts. He concocted several scenarios, but each seemed to be weighted against someone he for sure didn't want to send away.

Finally, what he considered the perfect plan occurred to him. In a frenzy, he worked out the details, checked it twice, made a couple of calls, then folded the page of rules and stuffed it into his shirt pocket. He leaned back in his chair, pleased with himself. Didn't matter now who was first to leave. It would be fair, and the lady sent home would deserve it.

On Friday, the twenty-ninth day of March, after dinner and Audrey's excellent apple cobbler, from his place at the head of the table, he scooted his chair back then stood.

"Ladies, I want you to know, I've enjoyed the past month with you." He walked around to his right and stopped behind Marge's chair. "I'm sure you're all wondering who's going home in a couple of days." She squirmed. He patted her shoulders then moved down and stood behind Virginia.

From across the table, Charlotte sat back in her chair. "Will whoever it is be leaving on Sunday?"

Dorothy looked around the table then turned to face him. "Have you already, you know, decided who?"

"Yes, I've arranged a car to be here at seven Sunday morning, and no, it hasn't been decided who will go. This is First Monday Trade Days weekend in Canton." He nodded toward his foreman. "Jorje."

The *hombre* passed out sealed envelopes to the women.

Preston smiled at each in turn as they questioned him with their eyes. "You'll find your first month's wages plus five hundred cash." He walked on around the table pausing behind each woman, touching her shoulder or hair.

"Two limos will be here at nine in the morning to pick you up. The same two'll bring you back at six. Don't be late on either end." He walked around to Vicki and barely caressed the back of her neck with the side of his finger. "What you buy or don't buy will determine who gets sent home."

He took his place at the head of the table then patted his shirt pocket. "I have a system already mapped out. Whoever scores lowest—" He gritted his teeth then ran his finger like a blade across his throat.

Vicki swallowed, let out a deep breath, then held out her hand. "May I have a look now?" she asked dreamily then winked. "You know I'm not my best in the mornings."

He laughed. "No, darling. That would defeat the purpose. You don't get to know until after you're through."

"But," Dorothy jumped up. "That's not fair, Dub."

"Why not?"

"How will we know what to buy?"

He shrugged. "You don't have to buy anything, save the money if you want. Enjoy the ride." He patted his pocket. "That may score you high enough not to get sent home, but it could also be a one-way ticket." He pulled out the folded page of rules. "I suggest you do what I hired you to do, be yourselves." He held up one finger. "But even if it's not your style, I need you to write down every penny you spend."

Natalie raised her hand. "What is First Monday?"

"Only the biggest flea market in the world."

"Really? Oh, fun."

The next morning as promised, a pair of stretched-out, midnight black, trimmed in gold Cadillacs arrived at eight forty-five. Audrey hung back while the first car loaded then climbed in last into the second. Once they turned off the property, she faced Vicki who sat next to her.

"So, any ideas about what he's after?"

The boy-toy shook her head. "Not a clue." She shrugged. "I don't know whether to buy something for him or me or the other women or nothing at all."

Natalie, who sat across from Vicki, smiled. "I think I, at least, have an idea of what he wants."

"Don't suppose you want to share what you think and why."

The exotic beauty giggled then crossed her legs Indian style beneath her. "Well, we've all been watching his every move almost a month now. If you don't know the man by now, you never will, but I'm figuring if you buy him something he doesn't have, you've bought yourself another month."

Virginia, who hardly ever said anything, shook her head. "Wrong answer."

The raven-haired beauty huffed. "So I guess you have this shopping spree all figured out?"

"No, I don't. Actually, I'd suggest we call on our resident researcher to tell us what she knows about the first Mrs. Preston." The once-upon-a-time ballerina nodded toward Vicki.

Audrey clapped her hands. "That's it. He knows what Nancy would buy, so—" She gave Vicki a springboard to spill her guts, but when the girl remained silent, she asked right out. "So, what did you find out about number one?"

"Lots of charity work, into her church." Vicki shook her head. "That's about all I remember. I was digging up info on him, not her." She pouted both lips and shrugged. "Gosh, I just don't know." She rubbed her head several times then snapped her fingers. "Hey, I do remember something. She especially liked green."

"You sure?"

"Absolutely. There was an article in the Tyler paper about him special ordering her a new green Cadillac. It had to be green, which was a big deal 'cause they didn't have a green one that year."

Everyone tried to talk at once, then Audrey hollered. "Wait a minute." Her words echoed, followed by silence. "What if green's a negative?"

"Couldn't be," Virginia stated as though she knew it to be a fact.

"How can you be so sure?"

"Logic. He loved Nancy so much that he waited five years to even look for another woman."

"So?"

"So? Are you blind and dumb? If she really loved green,

then it's at least a neutral, more than likely, a plus. Either way, you can take it to the bank I'll come back with something green, that is if I buy anything at all." Virginia shrugged then looked out the window as if all that needed to had been said.

Audrey reached over and tapped her knee. For a moment Virginia didn't respond then slowly turned around, rubbed her knee where she'd been touched, then looked up. "Yes?"

"Sorry." No response. "You serious about not spending any money?"

"You heard him. Hanging on to what you've got might get you another month."

Vicki bounced the L-sign on her forehead a couple of times. "Not this girl. If I lose, it won't be because I didn't shop my heart out. I'll go down in a blaze of goodie bags."

This once, Audrey had to agree. He obviously intended for them to reveal more about themselves by what they bought. At least that's how she saw it. Vicki and Natalie rehashed what had been said, while Virginia stared out the window. Audrey wasn't sure exactly what she'd buy, but one certainty surfaced like cream to the top, something would be green.

While the women shopped the world's biggest, oldest, and grandest flea market, Preston meandered around the place accomplishing nothing. All morning he kept redoing whatever task he assigned himself, then finally a little after noon, gave up and retreated to his office. He opened his journal and studied his notes. He hated the thought of having to send anyone home, but that was the deal, and he didn't think he wanted to see what would develop if they all stayed the entire time.

Each in turn, he pictured the ladies then made a list in his journal of what he liked and disliked. Not one of the eight had more negatives than positives. Too bad he couldn't keep them all, but then he didn't live in Salt Lake City.

If someone held a gun to his head right now, he knew who he would pick to leave, but they were all appealing. He'd still trust Lady Luck to see him through on this venture. One thing, though—he knew which one he thought he wanted, but if she didn't work out—he would marry one of them. He'd slept alone too long, and they were too fine for him to throw them all back.

After what seemed liked a week, the limos finally pulled into the drive. He stood back as his ladies unloaded then filed past with wide smiles and grins. He greeted each in turn, checking for expenditure lists, then followed the last one all the way into the kitchen.

When they all were seated with their booty tucked around, he took his place at the head of the table. "I see everyone made it back on time."

They all quieted.

He filled his lungs then let it out slow. "Each of you signed a non-disclosure agreement. That commitment follows you out of here. Now, legal's added a few new clauses so I'll get one more signature before you go, but I want whoever's sent home tomorrow to be aware that I will use whatever means necessary to enforce that contract." He looked at each woman in turn. No one looked away.

"Okay." He clapped once then rubbed his hands together then pulled the rules from his shirt pocket and unfolded them. "Swap your list with whoever's across from you. I don't want the loser to think this tally wasn't fair. And before we get started here, I want you ladies to know that I had a bad day. Just the thought of someone having to leave hurts my heart, but I can't marry you all. And today I decided one of you will be the next Mrs. W. G. Preston. That is, if one of you is agreeable when the time comes."

For a minute, it seemed like chaos, but soon enough, the women got the job done as requested. He would have had a good laugh if the stakes hadn't been so high.

"We all set?"

Everyone nodded.

"Plus ten points for an item with wood or rusty metal."

A few necks craned, and requests to see certain items were made.

"Plus twenty points for an item you bought with a cat on it."

Nods, several reached across the table to point out items with a feline to their scorekeeper.

"I'm curious, Dub. Why twenty points for cats?" Holly asked.

He stared at her a second, avoided looking at the cleavage her V-necked shirt revealed, then stated in a don't-be-asking-every-time voice. "Cats are low maintenance."

She nodded.

"Minus twenty for any item with a dog on it."

Vicki smiled. "Because dogs are needy?"

"Exactly."

"Plus thirty points for a green item."

A couple of the women exchanged knowing glances. He wondered why and waited while they checked and conferred then was asked to rule on an aqua scarf. "No, too blue."

"Minus thirty points for an item that's red."

Several moans preceded Dorothy jumping to her feet. "Now that's not fair, Dub. Why should that be a rule?"

"Why not?"

"Red's my favorite color."

"Sorry." He tapped the pages. "It's written right here, and

I'm not about to change the rules."

"But why red? It's the color of passion."

"Nancy hated red, okay?"

Audrey pulled Dorothy down.

"Plus forty points if you bought anything alive."

Vicki pushed her hair back from her forehead. "Is that forty for each?"

He glanced at the flat of flowers and lime-green shrubs by the kitchen door then smiled. "No, just the forty."

Marge leaned over and watched Vicki mark her score, adding the big four-0.

"Plus twenty points if you bought a gift for one of the other ladies."

Lots of awws and finger wagging took place back and forth across the table. Preston allowed himself a smile. It pleased him so many had bought something for the others.

"Minus twenty points if you bought anything for me."

Moans a-plenty.

"Plus thirty for an item over fifty years old."

More moans. Charlotte let out a little cheer.

"Minus forty points for anything plastic."

Dorothy shook her head, but said nothing, then looked away like her pet had died.

"Plus fifty points if you didn't spend any money except on food."

"Minus fifty if you have less than ten dollars left." He threw the paper on the table. "That's it. Total the scores, please."

The four pairs huddled to check and recheck. He tried to keep track, but couldn't. Finally it was all over but the telling.

"Marge, why don't we start with you?"

She nodded. "One hundred and seventy points."

"Eighty." Virginia stated in a low voice.

"Uh oh." Audrey shook her head. "Forty-five."

Dorothy fought back tears. "Well, I've enjoyed the month, you know. Because of the red and the plastic, I only ended up with fifteen points even though I did get everyone their own left-over container. Thought I'd put everyone's name on them. Of course, I got a red marker among my other red purchases."

"Don't give up just yet, Dot." Marge passed her a tissue via Audrey. "Someone could've even gone in the hole."

Holly shrugged. "Well, I've only got thirty." She made a pouty face. "That red shirt I bought Dub cost me fifty points."

Charlotte sighed. "Ninety for me, and I just thank the Lord for antiques!"

Natalie twirled her ponytail. "Sixty."

Preston faced Vicki who shook her head. "You know, I thought I was a goner, but even with your stupid rule about spending all of your money, I still have twenty points, I'll have you know." She turned to face the heavy-set woman she'd gotten off to such a bad start with. "Dorothy, may I be the first to say I hate to see you go? Truly. I don't know who's going to keep us organized when you're gone. I'll miss you. I really mean it."

Preston extended his hand, palm raised, toward Dorothy. "Could I see you in my office?"

CHAPTER EIGHT

Journal entry—March 31ˢᵗ
How in the world can anybody do that to themselves every day? It's gonna take me years to forget about how bad I feel right now.

That next morning, Sunday the last day of March, Marge rolled out of bed at four-thirty, threw on her robe and hurried to the kitchen. Preston sat at the head of the table sipping coffee. She grabbed a mug and joined him.

"You sleep at all?"

"No."

"Well, don't be beating yourself over the head, Buck."

He smiled. "You remembered. I was beginning to wonder."

"I kept forgetting when we were alone. My memory's not what it used to be." She wrapped her hands around the warm mug. "Anyway, the contest was fair. We all had the same chance."

"I know, but I still don't like it."

She started to say more, but instead quietly sat with him while he brooded. After several minutes of watching him watch the wallpaper, she took a sip. Her coffee had grown cold. She pointed at his. "Need a warm-up?"

He nodded at the refrigerator. "There's a pint of Jack

Daniels in the far corner behind the extra jar of pickles. Irish coffee seems appropriate."

She grabbed his cup, found the stashed whiskey, and poured him a fifty-fifty mixture with a dash of sweet cream before his words quit echoing in the cavernous kitchen. He sipped once then took a gulp of the lukewarm mixture. A wicked little grin crossed his full lips. "I thought it poetic that plastic did Dorothy in."

"Really? Why's that?"

"Hard woman. Plastic's hard."

She nodded. "Why, pray tell—if you don't mind me asking—did you invite her in the first place?"

He drained his coffee and slid the cup toward her. "When I was twelve, I spent an afternoon at my great-grandparents' farm."

She took it and headed for the coffeepot. "Go on. I'm listening." She poured the cup half full then reached for the liquor.

"A distant cousin I hadn't seen in years was there. Her name was Rebecca."

Marge set the Irish coffee in front of him, got comfortable, then sipped her own straight coffee. After the second gulp, he smiled then drained the mug again and slid it back to her. She caught it, but didn't move.

"While the grownups visited in the house, we were out in the barn." He glanced at the refrigerator.

She retraced her steps then set another fresh cup in front of him. After a long pull of the spiked brew, he smiled. "Dorothy could have been Becky all grown up." He waved his hand. "That and I liked the shape of her mouth." He stood, took her mug and his, then strolled to the counter and proceeded to brew another pot. Shortly, he returned with the whiskey, cream, and a carafe. He filled her cup with black coffee then mixed himself another. After a couple of sips, he leaned back. "I still think about that afternoon with Becky."

Marge's cheeks burned. She looked away.

He touched her forearm. "What's wrong?"

She shook her head, but didn't look at him. "Nothing."

He didn't say anything for more than a minute, then chuckled.

She faced him. "Don't laugh at me."

"Why not? You thought I was about to tell you some lurid tale of me losing my virginity."

"Well, weren't you?"

"No. I think about that day a lot because it was a comedy of errors." He drained his cup, re-mixed another, then smiled a cocky I-fooled-you. "Becky fancied herself a wild bull rider."

"A bull rider?"

"You heard right. She'd been riding some semi-tame, half-grown calves at her grandfather's, and figured she was ready for the real deal."

"You're both twelve, and she wants to ride a bull?" Marge leaned forward with her elbows on the table. "She must've been a wild child all right."

"Yep." His head bobbed, then he took another sip. "Said she was ready, so I herded a mean looking yearling into the squeeze chute and threw a rope around it. Keep in mind this was a thousand-pound animal, not a sweet fluffy calf." He took another long drink, then stared off like he could see it all in his mind's eye.

"She got astride that beast, but when I opened the gate, she chickened out and grabbed wood." He shrugged. "I had to tell my grandmother what happened because the rope was still around the calf." He grinned like a boy. "My great-grandfather, he must have been eighty, eighty-five, called those cows in and got that rope off. I figured he was going to whip us both. He must have thought about it, but in the end, he just laughed."

Preston looked off a second. "Last I saw him alive." He held his hand above his head and waved it around in a sloppy circle. "The money I inherited from him by way of my grandmother was the seed for what I've got today."

"And what happened to Rebecca?"

"Don't know. Never saw her again, either, not even at the old man's funeral."

"Why not?"

"She didn't show. Don't know why." He re-mixed his empty cup. "Then once my grandmother passed, I didn't hear much about that branch of the family."

"That's sad."

"I know." He closed his eyes and let his chin rest on his chest, then with a start, he jerked up. "We live our lives. Shame we can't keep in touch with all our family even if they are—what? Fifth cousins? Everyone's too busy."

Marge nodded, not knowing what else to do or say. She, too, had distant relatives she hadn't kept in touch with, but didn't everyone? He stared at the wallpaper again, apparently at least a sheet and a half into the wind. After several minutes of silence, he stated rather matter of factly. "For the longest, I thought I was in love with Becky. No one after her came close, until I met my Nancy."

"When was that?"

He shook his head and closed his eyes. "I was thirty, she was eighteen, and—"

Jorje burst into the room. "Limo's here early, Boss."

Preston focused on the intruder, and after a few seconds, nodded. "Okay. I'll get her." He pushed himself up, then wobbled down the hall. In a few minutes he returned carrying

Dorothy's bags. She followed close behind.

Marge hung back but followed them outside. The driver loaded the woman's luggage then took his seat behind the wheel. Preston held Dorothy's hands in his. "I hate it that you have to go."

"I know. Me, too."

"Let me know if you change your address. I'd like to send you an invitation to the wedding."

She nodded and managed a half smile.

He looked at her for a moment then leaned in. She rose on her tiptoes. He tilted his head and kissed her full on the lips. She kissed him back. For way longer than Marge was comfortable with, his lips lingered on Dorothy's.

Then she finally pushed herself away. "I wish things had been different, Dub."

"Me, too." He looked like he was trying to open his eyes wide and get her in focus using his nose as a site. "But I couldn't marry you all."

"I know."

He crossed his lips with a finger. "Keep our secret. Okay?"

She nodded. "I'll not breathe a word. Not for all the tea in China." She got into the limousine. "You can count on me."

"Knew I could." He looked back at Marge. "I knew it." Turning again, he blew Dorothy a kiss. "See you at the wedding."

"I wouldn't miss it for the world." She stuck her head out. "Bye, Marge. Good luck with this ol' bear."

"Goodbye, Dot."

He watched until the car disappeared, then turned back, took a step, and stumbled. Marge rushed to his side and steadied him. "I think we best get you to bed. What do you say?"

"Okay."

She herded him toward his office, figuring that the door behind his desk led to his bedroom. She figured right. Once past the massive oak desk and around the end of a rock wall, the hidden room revealed a king-sized bed, an oak chest of drawers, two computers—both with over-sized monitors and printers—a Ms. Pac-man game, and two dozen movie posters from the fifties and sixties plastered onto the walls.

She got him next to the bed and let go. He teetered back and forth once then grabbed her as he fell. She landed next to him. He smiled. "Do you love me?"

"You're drunk."

"Just a little."

"I'd say a lot."

He nodded. "I think that went rather well, don't you?"

"I didn't like it at all."

"Because I kissed her too long."

"Because you kissed her at all."

"You're right. I shouldn't have, but those lips of hers. And I thought she needed to be kissed."

Marge pushed herself up. He pulled her back down. "Stay with me."

She rolled off the bed and stood. "You're drunk."

"And you're beautiful."

She backed away and grinned. "Oh, stop it." Her cheeks warmed. "You'd think any woman was beautiful in your condition."

He shook his head. "No, I'm not that drunk." He held out his hand. "You haven't answered me. Love me yet?"

She backed to the door. "I don't know." She lingered just long enough to see the pain in his eyes, then hurried to her room.

CHAPTER NINE

Journal entry—March 31ˢᵗ
  Shame I can't change the past, but then she wouldn't be who she is. Maybe I can help shape her future.

Preston woke burrowed into his pillow. He wiped his face then attempted to focus his eyes on the clock that sat across the room on top of his dresser. After eight or twenty blinks, he figured out it showed two-eighteen. The afternoon sun, filtered by an oak tree's full branches, danced through the frosted panes of his shower. Daylight? He raised up. The pain behind his eyes knocked him back down. Why did he have on clothes? Oh, yeah.

"You drank too much," he moaned then rolled out of bed.

Between showering and dressing, it hit him. He'd dreamed about a woman, but it hadn't been Nancy. What had it been? Lust? Love? Or too much whiskey? He tried to recall exactly what happened in his dream, but the remembrance vanished without leaving one specific detail, only the knowledge that he had dreamed. He finished dressing then eased to his desk, retrieved his journal, and turned to her page. Before he could put pen to paper, his outer door opened.

"Bee man's here, Boss."

"I'll be right there. Don't let him unload any hives yet."

Jorje shrugged. "No worry there. That old man ain't doing nothing until he gets paid."

In spite of his headache, Preston stood. A wrecking ball pounded against his temples. "Seems to me if I'd been doing business with someone for better than ten years, I could muster some faith."

"Why should he? He always gets his money first."

Preston nodded. Jorje had a point.

Vicki had been sitting on the back porch when the old man rolled into the circle drive in an ancient, beat-up pickup. She stopped thumbing through an old *Life* magazine she'd bought in Canton and walked toward the driver's side. She stopped only a few feet from what appeared to be beehives.

"What's in the back of your truck?"

The old guy squinted one eye shut, spit a stream of tobacco juice out his window, then smiled a toothless grin. "Beehives." He opened the door, stepped out, and looked around. "Where's your daddy?"

She nodded toward the house. "Last I heard, Mr. Preston was taking a nap."

"How about hurrying him up some. Time's a wasting."

The door flung open. Preston strode toward the truck with Jorje hot on his heels. "Jake, I'm only counting twelve hives. Where's the rest?"

"Ain't no rest. Twelve's what you always get."

Preston shook his head. "I told you last spring when you picked up your bees to bring me fifteen hives this year."

The old man spit. "You did no such thing."

"You sure?"

He nodded then stuck out his hand. "Where's my money?"

"Take a check?"

"You know better than that. I don't truck with nothing but train riding, cash money."

Vicki stepped closer to her employer. Unsure where this was heading, she didn't want to even appear to be on the old geezer's side.

Preston stuck his hands in his back pockets and stared at the beekeeper. "Didn't I tell you last year not to be coming back unless I was getting credit?"

"Look, if you want to lease my bees, cough up some green backs, joker."

Vicki stepped in behind Dub who laughed then pulled a wad of bills from his pocket and handed it to the bee man. "Jorje, get our truck. Vicki and I'll ride with old Jake here."

He grabbed her hand, pulled her around the back of the old pick-up, then held the door while she slipped in and scooted toward the middle. Once the truck lurched forward, she lifted Preston's arm and sidled in tight. Pressing hard into his side felt good, like maybe being in the best place on earth. Nothing or no one could hurt her now.

She nudged his ribs with her shoulder. "Why you getting bees from this ol' cuss?"

Preston pointed. "Here's good for the first one." Jake slammed on the brakes, and the truck skidded to a dusty stop. Her boss jumped out then held his hand toward her. She let him pull her to the edge then waited for him to lift her down.

"I need the bees to cross-pollinate the apple trees. They should be in bloom any day now."

"Oh." She hung back while they unloaded the first hive. Dub stepped away a few feet while old Jake flipped open a wooden panel just under the top lip. Angry sounding bees swarmed out. She beat them both back to the truck then braced for take-off. The old guy must not have learned to use a clutch in all his years because he gave her whiplash—and a reason to hold onto Preston—every time he took off. No complaints.

She massaged her neck. "So, exactly where are your apple trees?" She leaned across to look out the window.

He laughed, put his cheek next to hers, then extended his arm and pointed toward the rows of vines growing on wire trellises. "There. I only grow dwarfs, and we train them to the wire."

The truck pulled out and hit a hole throwing her into him. She stayed pressed there for a second like a violet in a Bible before easing back to her seat. "How do you train a tree?"

"Lots of pruning." He waved at a head-high pile of brush. "That's from just this week. We've still got a lot more to do before the bloom."

"How interesting."

Eleven more times they stopped to unload the hives, and at each stop, Vicki asked more questions. She loved being with him, hearing the sound of his voice, looking into his baby blues. It had to be love. Too soon, the bee man left.

"So, where do all the apples we always have at the house come from?" Vicki climbed into the middle of the truck Jorje had followed them in.

Preston chuckled. "Don't you ever get tired of asking questions?"

"No. How can I learn anything if I don't ask questions?"

"Good point." He threw his chin south. "Take us to the warehouse."

She didn't know if it was Jorje's driving or the newer truck, but she sure appreciated the smoother ride. "Warehouse? You've got a warehouse here?"

"Sure. We ship apples and apple products all over the world." He looked smug like she should've known all this.

"You're kidding me, aren't you? Just like you were pulling

old Jake's leg awhile ago, right?"

"Well, I was funning the old man, but no, I'm not lying to you."

The truck rounded a turn, and a two-story tilt-wall warehouse that had to be at least twenty thousand square feet astounded her. Right out there in the middle of a field. "Man, who would have thought." She leaned forward. "How big is it?"

"Counting the chillers and office, thirty-two thousand."

"Wow. Can I see inside?"

"Sure."

Jorje parked the truck, then walked off without a word.

"Where's he going?"

Preston placed his hand on her back and herded her toward the front of the building. "Don't mind him."

"Oh, I don't. Matter of fact, I think it's kinda cute the way he looks out for you."

"Don't let him hear you say that."

"Why not?"

He unlocked the office, keyed the alarm, then flipped on the lights. "Cute and macho don't dance in my *amigo*'s book."

She nodded. "I'll remember that."

He led the way through the offices, then stopped. "Wait here while I go turn on the lights."

The sweet fragrance of apples pulled her through the opened door. It reminded her of Bath and Body's apple-fragranced lotions and spritzs. She stepped just inside and tried to follow him in the dark, but everything melded into dark gray shapes and shadows and kept her near the entrance. A far bank of lights came to life then in rapid succession the length of the warehouse lit up.

She strolled toward the closest pallet rack. From floor to

ceiling, shelves were loaded with wooden boxes. When he joined her, she pointed toward them. "What's in those?"

He pulled a large one down and opened it revealing a smaller wooden crate inside with six jars. "Apple butter, I believe." He pulled a jar out and handed it to her.

"All those boxes have jars of apple butter?"

"No." He pointed. "Those have jelly, those have juice." He grabbed her hand and pulled toward the back of the building. "Check this out."

She skipped along to keep up wishing the day would never end. No matter what happened, even if she was the next one to go, she'd always have this time with him to remember. He stopped in front of a stainless steel door with a long handle in the middle. "Can't keep the door open long, so when I open it, scoot inside."

She leaned forward and balled her fist like she was about to run a hundred-yard dash. "I'm ready."

When he yanked the handle, she dashed inside. He jumped in and closed the door behind him in one swift motion. The room, a good fifty-by-fifty was half filled with apples, crate after crate of apples.

"You grow them all?"

He nodded. "Every one. Right here on the place," then gave another nod toward the west. "We've got two more warehouses on the property where all the jelly, jam, juice, and butter's made."

She hugged herself. "Wow. Where are they?"

"Down the road a couple of miles. You can get to them the back way, too, though." He wrapped his arm around her. "Come on, we can't stay long."

"Oh, it's not that cold."

He opened the door and pushed her out. "It's low oxygen." He filled his lungs. "Keeps the apples from spoiling."

She pointed at another door. "Same thing?"

"Similar. It's a chiller, but we don't control the atmosphere in there."

"Why not?"

"Because." He held his hands up. "Don't you ever get tired of asking questions?"

"You're answering a question with a question, that's against the rules."

"Is it now? I thought I got to make the rules."

She started to use her little girl voice but stopped herself. "Not all the time. That wouldn't be any fun."

He slipped his hand into hers. "Come on. I bet Audrey's got dinner ready."

She didn't say anything until he locked the door. "Promise me something."

He looked into her eyes. "If I can."

She nodded, knowing he'd not commit to anything blind. She swallowed what she really wanted to say and blurted, "If you don't marry me, will you adopt me?"

He covered his mouth with his hand and closed his eyes, but she could see the grin anyway. He regained some control. "I guess I'm old enough to be your daddy. You got a mother picked out?"

She shrugged. "There's several acceptable, but Marge would do nicely."

"That she would." He nodded toward the passenger side of the truck. "Come on. I haven't eaten all day."

CHAPTER TEN

Journal entry—April 19th
  She's grace personified. I could watch her all day.

Contrary to Preston's prediction, the bloom didn't commence until the second week of April. The Galas flowered first, then the Empires' fragrant five-fold blooms burst forth. A delicate, crisp white soon blanketed the orchard looking from a distance like a magician's sheet hovering a few feet above ground. The sweet-scented cover rippled in the spring breeze. The ladies loved it, and even took to bringing picnic lunches out everyday.

Though things appeared to be running smoothly, all was not as it seemed. For all the white spread over the orchard, the bloom was just middling, and Preston couldn't decide if he should cull now or wait for the natural drop that should start in May and continue with the later varieties through June.

And with the ladies, two issues needed handling. Holly—in the room next to Virginia's—again voiced her concern for the lithe ballerina, and something was eating Audrey. Each day she slipped further into her funk.

By Friday afternoon he made the decision to leave the trees be, but not the women. Something should be done for them. He found the former ballerina in the kitchen working a crossword puzzle. As more often than not, she sat with her right leg sticking straight out at an odd angle. He watched her a minute while she pondered a clue, her pencil poised for when the word finally came, but apparently it didn't. She looked up. For a second, she stared, then her lips thinned into a weak smile. "Hi, Dub."

"Hi, yourself." He held out his hand. "Care to take a little walk?"

"I'd love to." She said, though her eyes carried no sparkle for proper punctuation.

He headed south toward his warehouse, but once past the first turn, pointed at a large boulder that guarded the footpath. "We can sit awhile if you'd rather."

"Thanks." She put her hand on the rock, pivoted on her left foot, then sat with her right leg sticking out straight.

He leaned his back against a tree on the other side of the path and put his hands in his pants pockets. "So, what's wrong?"

She shook her head. "Absolutely not a thing. Everything's wonderful."

He nodded toward her stiff leg. "That doesn't seem so wonderful. Well, it looks fine. I mean—exceptional actually, but—" He tried to extract his foot from his mouth. "What I'm trying to say is that your leg looks like it's giving you problems—pain."

She smiled and shrugged. "Oh, I just ignore it." She rubbed her thigh just above the knee. "It's been worse."

"Is that why you quit dancing?"

She nodded.

"Tell me about your mornings."

She looked away, shook her head ever so slowly, then looked back. "Have I done something wrong?"

He slipped in beside her aware of touching her shoulder to thigh. How long had it been since he'd enjoyed the feel of a woman's body so close? Virginia wasn't as soft as Nancy, but felt good just the same. He couldn't let her continue to suffer.

"No, of course not. But I don't like it that you hurt so bad. Some of the others hear you moaning. They're concerned—as I am." He put his arm around her. "Let me help you."

Audrey had been sitting on the back porch when Virginia and Preston strolled away. She told herself it didn't mean anything, that she shouldn't spy on them, but once they disappeared around the bend of the path, she couldn't stand it. Like she was going that way anyway, she eased on after them chiding herself for being a nosey-rosey. She rounded a cedar, spotted them sitting on the rock together, and jumped back behind the thick evergreen and peeked through the branches.

Why hadn't he taken her on any walks? It seemed he liked her more than just for her cooking, but the relationship appeared to be stuck on a plain of friendship and trust, and she wanted it to move to a more romantic level. She longed for walks alone with him and watching sunrises and moonlit dancing on the patio that lasted into the wee hours.

She couldn't hear their words, but when the talking stopped, he put his arm around Virginia, and she rested her head against his chest, cuddled into the crook of his shoulder. Audrey couldn't stand the sight of him and the dancer. She spun and raced to her room.

She hated this place and the conflicting emotions struggling within that kept her spiraling toward depression. Why were she and the other women playing this stupid game of his? And why had she grown to care one way or the other? Never thought she would. She signed on to get away from her boring life, collect her money, and spend the six months figuring out what she wanted to do next.

But who was she kidding? A man like Preston didn't come

along every day. She wanted him in her future. Somehow, she'd been swept into the competition.

Whatever led her to believe he would want someone like her anyway? And even if he ever did, he'd find out about Butch and—she threw her arms out to the side. All she could do was cook, and contrary to what the old wives claimed, the way to a man's heart obviously wasn't through his stomach, at least not if he had Preston's kind of money. But then he did tell her personal things. Oh, give it up, she told herself.

After sixteen teary daubs and two good nose blows, she pushed herself off her bed and trudged down the hall. If she didn't get something going in the kitchen, no one else would, and then he'd hate her for sure when dinnertime rolled around with nothing on the table.

She reached the foyer then froze. Preston sat in his chair at the head of the table—alone. He stared at a folded piece of newspaper. She wiped her eyes, pinched her cheeks, then strolled in like nothing was amiss. "Hey, Dub."

He looked up, tossed what appeared to be a half-worked crossword puzzle aside, then nodded. "Wondered where you were."

"Oh? Why's that?" She grabbed her apron from the kitchen hook and wrapped the strings backwards around her waist.

"Figured we needed to talk."

She fumbled with the bow, decided it needn't be perfect, then stepped closer. "What about?"

He nodded toward the chair next to him. "I was hoping you could tell me, Audrey."

Great. He had seen her spying. Now he would think she was a busybody, and she really wasn't. She'd only wanted to see where they were going. She started to blurt out a sorry, but he didn't look mad, concerned maybe, but not angry.

Could he be referring to something else? Dear Lord, it was almost the last of the month again. Surely, he wasn't going to tell her—

"I'm in the dark here, Dub. What do we need to talk about?"

"You, or more precisely, your state of mind. For the last couple of weeks, you haven't been yourself."

Slipping into Vicki's chair, she sat silent a moment and studied her fingernails. What could she say? She hated lying to him, but that's exactly what she'd done. And now her sins had found her out. Why had she been so stupid? She never dreamed it would be an issue. But if anything ever—well— he'd find out. Maybe she just hoped by the time he did, it wouldn't matter.

She looked into his eyes. "I'm sorry, Mr. Preston." She scooted the chair back. "If you'll be so kind as to call me a cab, I can be ready to leave in a half hour or so."

He grabbed her forearm and eased her back into her chair. "What in the world are you talking about?"

She grimaced. "The lie on my application. Isn't that—"

"You lied?"

"Yes. I have a tattoo, and I didn't want to tell you."

"Really? Of what?"

She ducked her head. "A guy's name."

He smiled. "How old were you?"

"Twenty."

He patted her hand. "I'm not going to send you home because of that."

"But you are sending me home?"

Just then Charlotte walked in with an armload of dirty bed linens. She must have heard. "Ooops, sorry you all. I was just on my way to the laundry room. Didn't mean to interrupt." She ducked out just as fast.

92

"So are you? Sending me home?"

"Heavens, no."

She sat back in her chair relieved. He wasn't making her leave. But he probably would now because she couldn't stand not coming totally clean since the door had been opened. "It's worse."

He laughed. "How's that?"

"The guy was my husband—well, for a few months, anyway. I lied about never being married, too."

"I see. So is there anything else I need to know?"

She shook her head. "I figured you'd never pick me, so you'd never find out, but then how could I explain about having Butch tattooed on my derriere if we ever—" She shrugged and grimaced. "—got naked together."

"That would have been a problem."

Did she detect a twinkle in his eye or more? She would assume nothing. "So will you call me that cab now?"

"No."

"Really?"

"Really."

Whew. She jumped to her feet. "Fabulous. What do you want for dinner?"

He smiled. "When I came in and found the oven cold, I ordered pizza. It should be here any minute."

Sure enough, seventeen minutes later, a young guy balancing four large steaming boxes appeared at the front door. Five minutes after that, Audrey had rounded up the other ladies and the junk-food chow-down commenced. Once the leftover pie was stored, Preston asked everyone to return to their seats.

"Ladies, there are two things you need to know. One, Virginia will be leaving in the morning."

Several tried to talk at once. "She," he said over the din, "is taking a medical leave."

Holly held up a hand like she was in school or something, but the others quieted, so she pulled it back down and spoke. "What does that mean?"

"She's going to Dallas to have her knee fixed and may or may not return. Depends on how long the rehab takes."

"Oh."

"Also I've decided how the next one to leave will be determined." He reached into his back pocket, pulled out an unwrapped deck of cards, and tossed them on the table. "Everyone but Virginia claimed to be a game player on their application. So now that she's on medical leave, we're going to play some cards to see who's the next one to be laid off."

Vicki grabbed the deck. "So that's what we're calling it now."

"Why not? That's what's happening."

She peeled off the cellophane wrapper. "I wonder if Dorothy filed for unemployment?"

"I don't think she worked long enough to qualify, but I could be wrong."

Several spoke at once, some to him, some to Virginia. He held up his hands. "Unemployment doesn't matter." He took the newly opened deck from Vicki. "A week from next Monday will be the last day of April. In addition to your check, there will be another five hundred cash in your envelope. At noon, we'll start playing poker. At the stroke of midnight, if no one's lost all her money, we'll count up. Whoever has the least will leave at seven the next morning."

The women checked each other's reactions. Holly lowered her forehead to the table then looked up. "So should we all pack just in case? I mean from a game that lasts until midnight to leaving at seven in the morning doesn't give a gal much time, you know."

"Okay, then. We'll make it first one out or count up at ten."

Marge took the cards from him. "We as in just the ladies, or we as in you, too?"

He chuckled. "I'll be playing. Wouldn't miss this game for all the apples in Washington State."

"What happens if you're the first one to go broke?"

"Won't happen."

"But what if it does?"

He nodded and smiled. "Then no one goes home this month."

Natalie shook her head. "This isn't fair, Dub."

"Why not?"

She twirled her ponytail. "I don't want to sound like a horse's patoo, but Virginia's leaving, yet may be coming back. She doesn't have to play at all, and that doesn't seem right—at least to me." The pixie looked around the table obviously looking for support.

"Seems fair to me." He eyed the other women. No one else appeared to have an objection. "I suggest between now and then you practice, but on the other hand, that might tip off how good or bad you are to the other ladies." He shrugged. "Your call."

"What rules?" Vicki asked.

"Dealer's choice and ante."

"Limit?"

"None."

"So if I want to play Dr. Pepper or baseball or high Chicago with low hold card wild, that's fine?"

He nodded. "If you must, but as I said it's dealer choice, and dealer ante, so if you make it too wild then no one will play with you."

She flicked her eyebrows a la Groucho Marx then smiled. "Do we get to keep our winnings?"

"Yes, darling, we'll be playing for keeps."

95

Chapter Eleven

Journal entry—April 27th
Got to watch her some today while she was working. I love
the way she can focus on the task at hand. Remarkable. I was
hoping she'd notice me watching, but she never did.

The plumbago Marge picked up in Canton flowered profusely
with blue clusters that brought a little heaven right down to
those front entrance beds. The two women thought Preston
hadn't bothered with the looks of them because he never left the
place since Nancy's death—never much saw the entrance. Jorje,
on the other hand, knew better than to mention what once had
been Nancy Preston's favorite pet project.

With the recent cultivation and a fertilizer, the new resident gardeners coaxed fragile lime green growth to cover the
dwarf nandinas that thrived behind the delicate blue flower
balls. An interesting contrast, especially with the bright
Gerber daisies. The leased bees loved it, too, darting in and
out as though ten acres of apple blossoms weren't enough to
pollinate. And between the tiny buzzers, butterflies fluttered
by kissing all the flowers and delighting the ladies.

Holly grabbed the next-to-last bunch of weeds, leaned
back, rolled her shoulders, then faced her gardening buddy.
"Oh, my aching back. I'll tell you, the first thing I'll be doing
if I'm the next Mrs. Preston is to have a breast reduction. I

never meant for them to be this heavy."

"Oh, really?" Marge pulled out the last weed by its roots then adjusted her broad-rimmed straw hat. "You had them enlarged?"

"Right before we came."

"I see. I have heard that does often help with aching backs, but that working in the dirt releases endorphins to help pain, too. I hear tell in Japan that land's at such a premium, city folks actually pay to get their fingers dirty."

"Well, I've always enjoyed gardening, pain or no. I just love the smell of the earth. And making things prettier."

"Me, too." Marge nodded toward a car coming down the farm-to-market, and the driver tooted his horn as he approached.

He slowed. "Good job, ladies. Been watchin' yer progress." He gave a wide smile, a wave, then eased on off.

"Thanks." Holly waved back. She loved the friendliness of country folks, put her in mind of her childhood days. It tickled her that the old codger admitted he'd been watching them all along. She'd seen him pass more than a couple of times before. "And see?" She chuckled. "It's a hobby so many others can enjoy, too."

The older woman gathered the tools in a bucket, then pushed herself up. Poor thing's knees must hurt. She sure seemed stiff. "You're preaching to the choir, because I agree and freely confess I love it, too. Mama's responsible for my green thumb. I teased her of being a walking plant encyclopedia and the reason I still enjoyed digging and making mud pies." She backed up a few steps and studied their handy work. "Looks good. I like it."

Holly joined her. "So do I. Job well done, partner."

Marge smiled, admired their handy work for another minute, then nodded toward the house. "Did you hear

Vicki's trying to get a game up this afternoon? You much of a card player?"

Holly laughed. "Me? I took my first steps under a poker table, and Mama always said the only reason she even saw it was that she dropped a couple of her chips."

"Oh, dear. I hadn't been worried before, but this poker game might be the end of me."

"Why would you think that?" Holly took the bucket of tools from her. "You've played before, haven't you?"

"Oh yeah, I've played—a lot. But mostly penny-ante. I'd get so upset with my brother, uncle, and dad for trying to buy pots. I didn't like paying so much to see that next card. I still hate high bets. Can't stand to lose money that way. A dollar's a plenty big bet far as I'm concerned."

"Think of it as his money, because I can tell you right now, it'll definitely be high stakes. Count on that because Dub's a high stakes kind of guy."

A breeze whipped up, and Marge held her hat on. "I can't bare the thought of leaving." She held her face up to the wind with her eyes closed. "But if I lose, I know you'll look after these beds. That way maybe I can come to First Monday and drive by and see them." She took a deep breath then turned to face Holly and smiled. "Remember my days here. I've really come to love the place and all my new friends, too."

"Why Marge, what a sweet thing to say. With all the competition, I hadn't really thought of the others as friends, more like opponents instead." She followed the only grandmother among them up the drive. "Bet this card game of Preston's really brings out the claws, but I wouldn't worry. No way he's going to send you packin' this early. Or Audrey either. He'd miss her cookin' too much." She shaded her eyes and studied the dark gray clouds rolling in from the west. Lightning flashed inside them. "Rain will be good for our flowers."

"And the apples, too." The older woman's eyes widened, and she tilted her head. "I'd about guarantee the game won't be rigged. You don't know him if you think he'd cheat for anyone." She stopped and faced Holly. "Why, I believe he'd sooner cut off a finger than not keep his word, and if he says the first one out goes home Tuesday morning, then believe you me, whoever loses will be gone—no matter who it is."

Holly nodded, but didn't believe it. She'd seen the way he looked at Marge and Audrey, and, of course, Vicki. If the money wasn't so good and the work so no-work at all, she'd have already been down the road. "You may be right, but I figure he'll see that the one he wants to go loses."

"Now how would he be able to do that? I don't think so." Marge reached the back patio and opened the tool shed.

Holly started putting the tools away, each on its own hook or peg, then nodded toward the house. "Go ask Vicki. She told an interesting story about Dub this morning."

"Really, where was I?"

"I'm not sure. Might have been when you and Dub were looking at his trees, spooning amidst the blossoms." Holly wrinkled her nose.

Marge felt her cheeks warm past comfortable and waved her off. "Oh, please. Don't use that tone or make that face. As I remember, he invited the whole room."

"Yeah, looking right at you, and you were the only one dressed."

"So? That doesn't mean you couldn't have come."

"Whatever." Holly stepped toward the kitchen then faced her and smiled. "You playing or not?"

"Oh, I guess so. Better get all the practice I can." Marge followed the younger woman into the house then hung back while she joined the game in progress.

Vicki dealt a round then patted the extra chair next to her, the one Dub normally sat in. "Come on, Lady Bug." She reached over and coaxed a tiny red insect with black polka dots onto her finger. "Get a hundred dollars worth of chips and sit down. We can't pluck you if you don't light."

Marge smiled. The beauty only needed a visor and a white shirt with garters to be a riverboat gambler. Against her better judgement, she joined the game anyway. At first, she played ultra conservatively. If anyone bet more than a dollar—the lowest denomination, she folded. Ten or fifteen hands in, she caught a jack-high straight. She won that pot then three of the next five. By the time Audrey broke the game up to start supper, Marge had amassed two hundred twenty-three dollars profit, except it was only chips. But still, it bolstered her confidence.

As Vicki put the rack of poker chips into its temporary storage over the refrigerator, Marge remembered what Holly said. "So what's the story you told everyone this morning?"

She looked confused. "What story?"

"The one about Dub."

A door closed and heavy boots on wood echoed into the kitchen. Vicki closed the cabinet then glanced over her shoulder. "My room, five minutes."

"Shall we take separate routes?"

Vicki beamed. "Hey, Dub. Hard day?"

"About the same, and you?"

"Not bad." She wrapped her arm around Marge. "Lady Bug here was the big winner today."

Her cheeks warmed. "Oh, we weren't playing for keeps. Doesn't mean a thing."

He grabbed a bottle of spring water from the fridge then headed for his office. "See you gals at supper."

Vicki winked and scurried down the hall. Marge waited a

couple of minutes then cold-trailed the younger woman to her room. She sat in the chrome chair made on odd angles across from Vicki who sat Indian style on her bed. "So what's the story? And why all the secrecy?"

"Oh, I'm not real interested in Dub knowing that I've spent so much time researching him." She grabbed the large tie-dyed pillow from her Canton excursion, threw it behind her then scooted back and leaned against the wall. "Anyway, I dug up this old *Texas Monthly* story. I don't know how the reporter got him talking, but Preston evidently told the guy he won Nancy in a poker game."

"No."

"Yes." Vicki licked her lips. "Now the Mrs. told a different story, claimed they were already sweet on each other before Dub ever played in one of their big family poker games."

"No wonder he's going to send the loser home."

"See why I didn't want him to know?"

Marge agreed even though she'd love nothing better than to hear the story from the horse's mouth. Maybe she'd ask someday, but first she had to get past next Monday's game.

CHAPTER TWELVE

Journal entry—April 29th

She's a natural. Oh the fun we could have had plying the riverboat trade if we'd lived a couple of generations before. What a team we could have made.

Though he normally didn't eat before noon, Preston decided a big breakfast was in order on Monday. Half a pot of coffee after five, he got a wild hare to cook that breakfast himself. He started by spreading out a slab of honey-cured bacon in an over-sized cast-iron skillet then turning on the fire to the lowest setting. He loved his pig, but only if cooked right, and that meant real slow and real done.

With one eye on the bacon, he mixed up a batch of biscuits, from scratch, if you please. It surprised him that he still remembered how. Soon enough Marge, usually first to rise of the ladies, joined him, followed by Audrey. By false dawn they had gravy, grits, two kinds of melons, and a fruit salad to go with the bacon and biscuits.

Preston pointed toward the hall with his gravy-stirring spoon. "Hey, Marge, would you find out how everyone wants their eggs?"

Before he got his two specialty egg skillets good and hot, she returned. "Holly and Charlotte want over-easy. Natalie's scrambled."

102

"Got it. What about you and Vicki?"

"I'm over-medium, and Vicki just pulled the pillow over her face when I stuck my head in."

"She did?"

Marge nodded.

He pulled out the eggs then opened the refrigerator freezer door and grabbed a couple of ice cubes. For a second, he shook them in his hand, then headed toward the bedroom hall, but before he got halfway across the kitchen, he stopped, tossed the ice into the sink, then returned to his egg cooking.

"I hated having it done to me. She doesn't have to get up and eat this morning or any morning." He plopped a fat pat of butter into each of the small skillets.

"Well now, I'm glad you feel that way, Dub." Vicki strolled into the room, rumpled, but still glamorous. "I'll take mine blindfolded. And, uh, hold the lace if you don't mind."

He glanced at her bunny slippers then smiled. "Only because I like a woman who wears rabbits."

Three biscuits in, Preston figured he should stop, but everything tasted so good, and he hadn't even gotten around to the fruit salad yet. Finally, he pushed his plate back. "Anyone object to moving game time up? I say we play from nine to nine instead of waiting until ten to start."

Everyone agreed. Even though he'd done most of the cooking, he helped with clean up. He couldn't remember the last time he'd anticipated anything so much as this game. It amused him, and at the same time, caused some concern. Was he trusting Lady Luck too much? He knew who he didn't want to leave, but wasn't sure who he did, so maybe he didn't have a choice but to see what was in the cards.

Before nine, Jorje rolled in a felt covered poker table, then while Preston righted it and set the chairs, the foreman left again. He returned with a box loaded with manila envelopes.

As the clock's longest hand pointed straight toward heaven, Vicki, the last one, slipped in beside Preston. He smiled, then nodded toward his foreman. "Pass out the packets."

Jorje complied then disappeared.

"As promised, you'll find your check and five hundred in cash. First one to lose all their money, or who has the least amount at nine tonight—if we last that long—leaves here in the morning at seven sharp." He looked at each woman, and each one returned his gaze. "As I said before, remember you've each signed a non-disclosure agreement."

Vicki poked his arm. "Come on, Dub. We know all that. Let's play some poker."

He stared at her a second. She didn't look away, but did shrug an apology.

"Anyway, whoever has to leave, we'll talk right after the game." He took the deck Vicki had opened, shuffled them three times, then dealt them out face up. "First jack deals. Dealer antes."

Marge, who sat on Preston's right, didn't want to catch the first jack, but got it anyway. "How much am I suppose to ante?" She gathered the cards.

Preston shrugged. "Ten's fine."

She groaned, but tossed out the bill then slid the deck over for him to cut.

"Thin to win." He grinned.

She shook her head.

Marge wanted to proceed slowly like in her practice games, but fate denied her. She dealt herself two pair, opened for a dollar, then raked in the pot when everyone folded after the draw. She got her eleven back plus the six she won. Not much return. Maybe she bet too conservatively. A round of bad cards convinced her the original plan remained the best plan. She only needed more money than one lady at the end of the game.

By the noon break, she was about a hundred and fifty down. At this rate, the antes would break her. She wandered out to the patio, trying to formulate a plan. When she reached the pond, the goldfish swarmed toward her and opened their mouths. She'd seen them do it before, but it always amazed her they were so tame. One of the bigger ones, a solid gold that Preston called Roscoe, even let them stroke its back. She retrieved some food from under the bench and sprinkled a two-finger pinch.

"Not too much." Preston stepped beside her. "How you doing?"

"Not good. I'm a hundred and fifty down."

"Really? I had it at a buck thirty-eight."

She pulled the wad of money out of her skirt pocket and counted it, then counted it again. She put the money away then stared at him. "How did you know that?"

"I don't play the cards. I play the players."

His words didn't register. He stood too close, and even with so much at stake, she could only think about being sent away from him. She hated herself for being so foolish, but what could she do? She had to see this through to the end, or she'd never forgive herself.

His lips spread into a broad smile. "Unlike some people."

She focused. "So what you're saying is I'm not playing the players?"

"Exactly. You should know who's up and who's down, who can and can't be bluffed. There's very little luck in poker."

She nodded, but wasn't sure how his words of wisdom could save her. "So, how's everyone else doing?"

"Vicki and Holly are up. You, Natalie, Charlotte, and Audrey are all down."

"What about you?"

"Seventy-three up. Thank you very much for not calling my last bluff."

"When did you bluff me?"

He laughed. "I hear I have a tell sign, leastwise Vicki says I do."

She laughed with him. "So that's why you told Vicki there's no way you could lose?"

"Not this game. Not today."

She stared into his eyes a moment then had to look away, so she studied the fish instead. This game of his was worse than a horror movie, and she hated scary flicks. She could tell he cared about her. He even said she was beautiful, but here they were playing stupid poker to see if she had to go home or got to stay at least another month.

Tears welled, but she blinked them away. Crying wasn't the answer. She wiped her eyes then faced him. "I think us playing poker to see who goes home is a terrible thing to do, Dub. You should just pick someone if that's what you want to do, or just let everyone stay the six months you've guaranteed." She shook her head. "I've half-a-mind—" She stopped herself, then hurried inside. She didn't want to lose. She hated losing anyway, but for sure didn't want to lose this game and have to leave.

In a few minutes, Preston sauntered in and called everyone to the table. "I believe it's Natalie's deal."

For the next four hours, Marge did everything she could to play the other players, but her stack of green backs still dwindled painfully short. If her calculations held, she was the biggest of the losers. The only consolation was the four hours left to play. She might hit a good hand.

Preston ordered pizza then called a thirty-minute break at five-thirty when the pies arrived. Marge admitted things looked a little better. She had clawed her way back to only ninety-four dollars down. She grabbed two slices and a bottle of spring water then retreated for the patio. Maybe he'd join her again.

With only ten minutes left, she strolled back in. Preston, Vicki, and Audrey stood in a tight circle next to the refrigerator laughing. She started to join them, but decided she didn't fit in their little winners-only clutch. She slipped back into her seat at the table and gathered the cards. At five-fifty-eight, he returned to his chair.

Preston leaned close as the other ladies took there seats. "You're doing better."

She nodded. "Am I still the big loser?"

"It's close."

"I hate this."

"I know." He took the deck from her. "It's my deal." He flipped a ten to the center of the table.

With each tick of the clock, the rock in Marge's belly grew heavier. She'd win a little then lose it back a dollar or two at a time. The ten-dollar ante every seventh hand certainly didn't help her cause either.

By eight o'clock, she was beside herself. Two bad calls had about done her in. Both times she'd been certain Holly was bluffing, but the redhead held the winning hands. How could she play the players if she couldn't read them worth a flip? Oh well, maybe she'd lose and be done with his horrid scheme.

By eight-thirty, it had gotten worse. Two hundred eighteen dollars down, and if that wasn't bad enough, the deal came around to her again. Make that two hundred twenty-eight down. "Straight low-ball."

Why that came out of her mouth, she never knew. For

some strange reason, she called it. At least she'd get to look at five cards before making another bet. She dealt then leaned back and studied her hand. Great. Two pair, and she called straight low.

Preston opened for five dollars. Three called before Marge. For a few seconds, she studied the nasty pairs. She should probably fold, but instead, she laid her cards face down and pitched a twenty into the pot.

"I raise."

What was she thinking? Preston, Vicki, and Holly already called, and now, her big bet ran Audrey and Natalie out, and they were the ones she needed so badly to beat. Now what?

"Cards?"

Preston took one, Vicki one, and Holly two.

"I'm good." Marge heard the words come out of her mouth, but couldn't believe it. She was a sure loser holding two pair. Why did she stand pat? She might've at least had a chance. This would make her or break her, and she'd be done. It'd be over. No doubt Preston would see through her.

She tapped the table. "You opened, Dub."

"Check to the raise."

The other two tapped the table.

"No, not this hand." She tossed a fifty toward the center, then slipped her hands into her lap. Preston folded his cards almost before her fifty hit the pot. Was he being kind, or had he really not helped? Likewise, Vicki chunked her hand, leaving only Holly.

The redhead pulled a bill out of her stack and held it out, but didn't let it drop. Marge's face grew warm. She must be sweating bullets, but she resisted the urge to wipe her forehead. For way longer than she wanted, Holly stared at her. Marge stared right back, then gave her a little smile.

"I'd be a fool to call a pat hand. You haven't bluffed the

whole day. Don't know why I'm even considering it." She tossed her cards.

Marge raked in her winnings. That was a quick sixty bucks. Preston shuffled and dealt hold-em, his usual game. Marge won high hand with a flush and split the pot with Vicki. The next hand she folded early, but won the one after that with two pair.

Things didn't look quite so bleak, but she was still sixty-four dollars down with eighteen minutes to play. But Natalie and Charlotte had gained on their losses, too. Two hands in a row, Marge folded, then lost twenty. Her turn to deal always came around too soon. She pitched a ten out.

"Five card stud." She dealt one hold card and one up-card around. When she peeked at her down card, a one-eyed jack peeked back. He matched the one showing. All right. A pair of jacks.

"Natalie, your king's high."

"Check."

Holly tossed a five in the pot. "Get your checks at the bank, ladies."

Marge leaned over as if to examine Holly's card, the nine of hearts, then let her bill drop. She didn't want to make it so high as to run them out, but neither did she want it too cheap for them to try and draw out on her. "I raise. Twenty plays."

Vicki folded. "I would've stayed with you, Lady Bug, if you'd called that straight low again, but I haven't even got anything to draw at."

"You're forgiven." The others called the bet. "Pot's right."

The second up-cards flew around the table. "No help for Dub. Oh, another nine for Holly. Nine's a pair. Natalie gets a ten to go with her king, possible straight flush. And Charlotte? Another spade. A three for me? I need to bone up on my

109

dealing. So, then nines are new."

"Twenty's good." Holly tossed the Jackson onto the table.

"I call." Charlotte dropped two tens to the middle.

Marge called without comment. Preston folded.

"I'll call one more time." Natalie said in an off-hand way, but then couldn't seem to get her money out fast enough.

She dealt around again, but for some reason, Marge watched their eyes as the cards fell. No one's twinkled. Natalie caught Holly's nine right in front of her, and Holly got a six. Another spade fell on Charlotte's horde of black cards. Marge flipped her own card down on top of her last. A jack. Whew! She barely managed to swallowed her gasp.

"Pair of jacks are high." She hoped her voice sounded normal, but couldn't tell for sure with her heart pounding so loud. She counted out sixty dollars for all to see then shoved the money to the center of the table. "That's a twenty for each jack, ladies."

Natalie called. "Yeah, right."

Holly folded and Charlotte called. "You wouldn't be fibbin' now, would you Miss Marjorie?"

Marge only smiled sweetly and dealt the final fifth cards, face-up, Texas-style.

She tossed Natalie a queen of hearts. "There goes the flush, still a possible straight." The look in the woman's eyes chilled Marge.

She flipped Charlotte her card, another spade. Oh dear? What had she done? She flipped over her card, then leaned back. What was she going to do? They both had her beat.

Charlotte pointed to her. "You going to bet those two pair or what?"

Marge looked down and spread her cards. A three! She got another three! She did have two pair, but with the jacks being trips, she held a full house. Oh, wow. She had them both beat. She sighed a thank-you prayer that she wouldn't be going anywhere then shrugged. "I'll check to the straight and the flush."

Natalie glanced at Charlotte's cards then knocked the table. "Check's good."

"Oh, no, girls. Not with me." Charlotte pitched a hundred into the pot.

Preston leaned forward. "Now this is getting interesting."

Marge nodded. A gray cloud moved in over her because now she was sure who would be going home. "Call."

Natalie shook her head from side to side. "If you can, I can't." She folded her cards.

Marge turned over her hidden jack. "Full house."

Charlotte jumped to her feet and leaned over the table. "Why in the world did you check a full house?"

"I knew I'd won enough, figured I'd let you two decide who lost."

Four minutes remained on the clock, so Preston dealt another hand. Marge folded without looking at her cards, and Vicki took another seventy dollars from Charlotte. At the stroke of nine, Preston stood. "Charlotte would you be so kind as to join me in my office after everyone counts up."

CHAPTER THIRTEEN

Journal entry—April 29th
Can lightning strike twice? Apparently so. What fire.

Marge arranged her money in hundred dollar stacks, but no one asked her how much she had. Plainly, Charlotte was the big loser. The poor woman's eyes glistened with unshed tears, but she held her chin high. She pitifully chided Natalie into going through the motions of counting up.

'What if' danced through Marge's heart. What if she lost? Would it be the end of her relationship with Preston? Not that she really even had one. Well, he liked her, she was certain of that if she knew anything at all. But was whatever had grown between them so precarious, so fragile and meaningless, that a stupid poker game could end it?

Her heart broke for the Southern Belle. The absurdity of Preston's games coupled with Charlotte's anguish caused an avalanche of angry thoughts that slammed Marge head-on and took her breath away. Her face burned, and her chest tightened. She jumped to her feet then marched to his office. Her balled fist stopped inches from his door. On second consideration, she knocked two raps with a single knuckle.

"Come in."

She stepped around the door, closed it behind her, but

kept hold of the knob. Where could she start? She couldn't make herself speak.

He sprang from his chair and rounded his desk. "What's the matter?"

She threw her hands up. "You. This game you're playing. Making us play." He stopped at the edge of his desk. She dropped her hands and her head. Then she looked him in the eye. "I hate it."

"I know." He looked at his shoes then back with a sigh. "You've told me already."

First words, then phrases ran through her mind, but none of them reached her mouth. She wanted to tell him she was through, volunteer to take Charlotte's place, but she couldn't stand to throw away whatever time she might have with him. If only another month, she still wanted it. "Why can't we all stay through the guarantee period?"

He shook his head as though shaking off the idea. "Sorry, that's not the deal. I said I'd send one home a month. That's how it's got to be."

She hated being on borrowed time. "But why?"

He ran his hand over his mouth. "You're as bad as Vicki."

"What does 'Darling' have to do with this?" Oh she immediately wished she hadn't said that. Now he'd think she was jealous.

He grinned. "She's always asking questions, too."

One part of Marge wanted to slap that smirky smile off his face and another longed to kiss it away from his full lips. Had she gone insane? "You also said that if we'd have you, you were going to marry one of us."

"That I did."

She opened the door. "Then it seems to me, as prospective-wives, we deserve to know why you're doing it this way." She

113

slipped out and closed the door before he could smart off again.

Preston had to agree. Marge and the other ladies probably did deserve an explanation. A second tap on his door pulled him back to the task at hand. "Come in."

Charlotte walked through with her head held high. "You wanted to see me?"

He gestured toward the left wingback then slipped around to his own chair. "I've got a couple of documents I'd like you to sign, then you'll get your check."

"No problem."

"Sorry you lost the game."

"Guess that's the way it goes. I was looking forward to antiquing with you. Maybe we could still go sometime."

"Maybe, or maybe you can do some shopping for me down the road." He pulled the legal forms from a folder in his file drawer. "You going back to North Carolina?"

"Not just yet. Thought I might snoop around the Metroplex awhile. Texas has always been like a fairytale land to me. You know, all the cowboys and Indians and all. Might even go see the capital and Houston since I'm so close."

"Well, I hope you'll hang around long enough for the wedding, then. I'm curious, who do you think I should pick?"

She looked away, then back, and smiled. "Why, me, of course."

He rewarded her humor with a chuckle. "Besides you."

"Well, I don't rightly know for sure, but I can truly say with conviction that you'd be making a mistake with Vicki."

"Really? Why do you think that?"

"Age, for one. Besides that, she's nothing but a gold digger."

A quick nod indicated he might agree, even though he

knew better. He slid two pieces of paper toward her. "You know lawyers love their mumbo jumbo. Read it twice if you need, but it's basically a repeat of the don't-tell-anyone-what's-going-on-here you signed in the beginning. Except this one more clearly specifies the penalties."

She studied the papers only a minute then looked up. A tear ran down her cheek. She swiped at it. "Dub, I'd never—"

"I know. I do, but just in case, I need you to sign."

She took a pen from his desk and signed both pages without reading further. "Of course." She stared a minute at the sixteen thousand-dollar check then slipped it into her pocket. "There's no one could ever accuse you of being a cheapskate, Dub." She swallowed hard and looked him in the eye. "I never ever thought I'd be going home next. Can I have my goodbye kiss now, or do I have to wait until tomorrow morning?"

He leaned back and studied a spot six inches over her head. Marge had been right. He never should have kissed Dorothy. But then what was the harm? He stood. "Now's fine."

She scampered around his desk and into his arms, wrapping hers around him. She licked her lips, stretched up on her tiptoes, then tilted her head back. He kissed her, soft at first, then responded with more passion than he intended, rather enjoying her pressed hard against him.

When he pulled back, she pressed in, buried her head against his chest, and squeezed his middle tight. Deep inside, a spark flickered, some long-dormant fire ignited after those many years. He leaned back. It had been too long.

She slithered off his chest and backed away to arm's length. Her eyes sparkled as she nodded toward his bedroom, then slipped her hand into his. She tugged a little, but he didn't budge.

"Wouldn't be right."

She closed her eyes, pouted her bottom lip, then nodded slowly. "I know, but—" She let go of his hand, wiped her cheek, then smiled. "I want you to know I had lots of fun being here, Dub, and I'll never forget you."

"Keep in touch. I'd like to see you at the wedding."

"Oh, you can count on me being there. Just let me know when and where." She patted her pocket, the one where she stashed the check. "Will I see you in the morning?"

"I'll be around."

She backed to the door, blew him a kiss, then disappeared.

He licked his lips, and promised himself that he'd remember how she tasted, the light touch of her lips, the hint of peach. He shook his head. Shame he couldn't have been born a sultan. No, he could only choose one, only marry one. Actually, one was all he wanted. That is, if the one was still game once the game was over.

The merry month of May arrived. That's what Nancy always called it, then she'd burst into song. Preston was pretty sure it was from a musical, but wouldn't have been able to name that tune for double his riches. For the first three weeks, he couldn't settle on the next way to decide who went home.

He was beginning to dislike this game a little himself. Then with only four days to go, fortune interceded. A button popped off of his favorite work shirt. He retrieved the small disc of bone then placed it and the shirt on his dresser.

The idea, unlike most, didn't jump on him in a flash. Instead, it seeped in as he studied the button. Before he realized what happened, he'd claimed the thought as his own. Then he spent a while pondering the ramifications. Clad only in his T-shirt and underwear, he marched to his desk and put his new plan into action.

After dinner that same evening, he lingered at the table while the ladies cleaned up, then asked Vicki to hold up on starting the dishwasher and invited them all back.

"I've decided what we're going to do next." He nodded at Marge. "And I've been asked to explain why I'm doing this the way I am."

"In the morning, you're all going to Dallas." He rocked back in his chair and waited. The silence circled like a lone turkey vulture signaling the flock, then the ladies couldn't stand it any longer.

"What for?" Vicki's velvety alto drowned out the others as they all talked over each other.

"A little shopping and whatever else you want."

"You sure must want a wife who's a good shopper, Dub."

"Thought that's what all wives loved to do."

She smiled. "So, can we party all night and sleep all day?"

"If that's what you want, but I don't think that'll get you another month."

Marge sighed. "So this is another contest?"

"Of sorts, I guess." He patted his shirt pocket. "But with another set of rules."

Vicki held out her hand. "Do we get a peek?"

"No, but this trip, you buy for me."

"For you? Like what?" Vicki seemed to have appointed herself spokesperson.

"Whatever you think I need."

"What about wants?"

"What about them?"

Natalie grabbed Vicki's arm. "He's not going to tell us, are you, Dub?"

"Smart lady." He smiled. "I will tell you this. What you do or don't do when you're not shopping will count half or more of your score."

117

Holly raised her hand. "What kind of budget are we on?"

"My bank's overnighting a MasterCard for each of you. It'll have a five thousand limit." He stared at Vicki. "Don't be going over."

She threw her hands up as if Hayden Tilden from LAWDOG, the new novel he was reading, had hollered stick 'em up. "Wouldn't dream of it. Not me, not after Canton."

"Good, now, as to the why." He looked at each in turn, starting with Vicki to his left and ending with Marge. "When I was thirty, I met Nancy who was eighteen." He shook his head. "The economy had tanked, and I couldn't get a job off-shore, so I went to work for the railroad.

"Lived in an apartment in Oak Cliff. Just so happened my Nancy's grandparents lived in the same complex. She and I met one Saturday at the pool." He held up his index finger then swiped a slash in the air. "First stroke of luck. Had a flat that morning or I'd have gone over to a buddy's house and missed her." He added a second slash.

"Her uncle happened to be late that evening when I walked her back to her grandparents' apartment, so his chair at this big family poker game they had going was empty." He drew the third imaginary notch. "A little after midnight, I caught a good hand, Nancy's father thought he had one better." A fourth slash.

"When he couldn't call the last hundred I bet, I told him his permission for me to date his daughter was good enough to call my bet." He laughed. With an angled swipe, he crossed the four imaginary sticks. "My four jacks beat his four nines, and the next thing you know, I'm watching him walk her down the aisle."

Vicki clapped her hands. "So you did win her in a card game."

He raised an eyebrow and stared at her. She ducked, obviously embarrassed. "Yeah, guess you could say that. She'd already told me he wouldn't let her date an old man like me, but that if he would say yes, she'd love to go out."

Marge shook her head. "Nice story, Dub, but what does that have to do with us?"

"Lady Luck—Dear Destiny, fortune or fate? Whatever you want to call it. The lack thereof sent Dorothy and Charlotte home."

"So because of one incident, you're trusting the rest of your life to luck."

"It isn't just one time." He waved his hand over his head. "Everything I've got is because of being in the right place at the right time. I inherited a little piece of money from my grandmother just when a guy I knew finagled a mineral lease on a thousand acres up in Oklahoma. If he'd hadn't been short of cash and needed my two grand to finish his well, I'd never've gotten in on that deal—or the next one, or the next."

He shook his head. "In no time, I'm buying up half the old leases in East Texas." He rocked back and filled his lungs.

Natalie leaned in. "Why'd you do that?"

He pointed to the floor. "I'd lucked into a little known fact. Under the shallow and played-out East Texas oil, a monstrous pocket of natural gas just waited to be let out."

Caught up in the story, Vicki spun around and faced Natalie. "It's called the smack-over." She turned back and nodded. "Right?"

"That's right, darling. All your library time wasn't wasted."

She gave the other women a sideways glance. "How'd you know?"

He winked then checked the wall clock. "I suggest you ladies get some sleep. The limo will be here at seven and will leave as soon as the credit cards arrive."

CHAPTER FOURTEEN

Journal entry—May 30th
Parting is not sweet sorrow, it's agony. Can't believe I let them go so far for so long.

Sleep. What bliss. If only Vicki could comply with Preston's suggestion to get some, she'd be more than pleased to, but for her, it didn't work that way. When most folk's bedtime rolled around, sleep flittered about like an illusive dragonfly that came—or left—of it's own accord.

A creature of the night, she could fall asleep as easily as an autumn leaf floated to the ground—so long as the sun shone brightly. After dark, a different story, and besides, until she figured out who was feeding the man all the tidbits of information that she didn't necessarily want him to know, she might not sleep at all.

She paced and pouted, scribbled a list in logical order, then analyzed what her gut told her. She hoped it had been Charlotte before she kissed him goodbye, but didn't really think so. The belle had been too busy trying to seduce him. So who could it be? The question dogged her until almost dawn, then as if someone had flipped a switch, she passed out.

"Wake up, dear."

A hand shook her shoulder. She opened one eye. "Lady Bug? What time is it?"

"Six-ten, and Dub's cooking breakfast. Want any eggs?"

She scooted up in the bed. "Sure. How long do I have?"

"Oh, I'd think at least fifteen minutes."

She swung both legs over the side, then stared at the older woman a moment. "You didn't tell him about the library, did you?"

"Goodness no. I wondered about that myself."

"Didn't think so, but I just couldn't get to sleep last night for all my wondering." She stretched then waved Marge out. "So anyway, thanks. I'm up, and I'll be there."

She glanced at her wrist. "Okay, dear. See you then."

With almost two minutes to spare, Vicki slipped into her seat. Marge and Preston helped Audrey with last minute preparations. The bacon, biscuits, grits, sliced tomatoes, and skillet of steaming gravy already loaded the table.

Preston set a stack of pancakes on one corner and her eggs—blindfolded and lace held—in front of her then slipped into his seat. "Morning. Glad you could make it."

She flipped him a smirky quarter-nod. Probably more than any man desired at this time of night. The one thing she hated about being here was all this nasty, too-early rising. She'd sleep until noon everyday if she had her druthers. "Is this like a last meal tradition or something?"

He laughed. She loved it when he laughed. "I guess you could call it that."

She leaned in to whisper in his ear. "I don't want a last meal."

"I know."

She started to ask for buying suggestions, but decided it might be on his rules list. She sure didn't want to start out to Dallas in the hole. "Not that I am, but asking for help is one of the negatives on your list, isn't it?"

He grimaced. "Am I so transparent?"

121

Audrey set another batch of pancakes on the opposite end and sat down. "Marge, want to bless the food?"

She did, then the man took to eating. Vicki loved the way he ate—with restrained gusto. She sipped her coffee and nibbled a biscuit, wondering exactly what he was after with this shopping trip to Dallas. That and the identity of her snitch, took turns on the center stage of her mind while everyone else seemed too busy eating to do much talking.

Once the pace slowed, and the conversation flowed beyond food, Vicki made herself focus. But before anything useful was said, Jorje strolled in with a UPS letter in his hand.

"This what you're looking for, Boss?"

Preston ripped it open. Five gold cards fell out. "I believe it is."

The Mexican jerked a thumb over his shoulder. "Limo's ready, too."

"Good." He stood, scooped up the cards, then held his arms out and motioned toward the door. "Let's go, ladies. Time for another adventure."

"Well, wait a minute. I have to get my purse."

"Me, too."

Chairs scraped the floor in a ruckus, and all the women scurried toward the bedroom hall.

"And I've got to get my shoes on. I'm not wearing rabbits to Big D." Vicki flashed him her sweetest, most innocent smile then followed the ladies.

At the car, one of the same stretched out Cadillacs as before, Preston waited by the opened door. He smiled as he handed out the cards. Vicki boarded last.

He stuck his head inside the door. "Pin number is the last four digits of your social security numbers. Get yourselves some cash. The car and hotel are already paid for." He looked at everyone in turn. "Write down every penny you spend and everywhere you go. Not being able to account for your time or money is bad."

No one responded.

"Okay. The car will leave Dallas at six sharp Thursday evening. Don't be late, and have fun."

Holly waved her new card. "We've got it."

"Good." He closed the door and stepped back.

Vicki studied the apple trees—except they were vines—as the limo eased along the lane. Once it turned onto the farm-to-market, she faced the other women. "So, who's the snitch?"

No one said anything, but neither did anyone look away.

"Come on, ladies. Someone's been talking to Dub, and I want to know who."

Again no one responded.

She looked at Marge. "Any ideas?"

The older woman shook her head. "I know nothing."

"Wait a minute." Natalie gazed out the window. "Why do you think it was one of us? It could just as easily have been Charlotte."

"Yeah, or Dorothy," Holly offered.

"Not Charlotte. You heard her. She was too busy doing everything she could to get him in bed. I don't think she would've said anything, didn't have time. Besides, ruining me was not on her mind."

"Well, as glad as I was to hear from her when she called from Billy Bob's, I can't believe she had the nerve to admit she went after him that way." Holly pulled her leg up under her. "Anyway, there's still Dot—or Virginia? Either one of them could've said something."

"Maybe, but I don't think so. They've both been gone too long, and he just mentioned it last night."

Holly held her hand up and waved it. "There's another plausible explanation."

"Like what?"

"Well, after he hired me and before we came in March, there were several times I thought I was being followed." She looked around. "Anyone else notice a lot of black sedans lurking around?"

Vicki shook her head. "I didn't. Why would he do that?"

Audrey patted Vicki's knee. "Wait a minute. Holly may have something here. Now that she's mentioned it, I thought a time or two someone was following me, but never thought of it being Preston. Anyway, nothing ever happened, so I chalked it up to paranoia. But I could see Dub checking us out."

Vicki leaned back. Maybe that's what it was. Maybe he'd hired PIs to follow the ladies around. She could imagine him doing it, too. What else had Preston hired his private snoops to do? How deep into her past had the goons dug? She hugged herself. What had he found out? Man, it didn't make a bit of difference what she bought him in Dallas. She was a goner for sure, and that broke her heart.

Marge watched the younger woman as she pondered this new revelation. After seeing the hurt in Vicki's eyes, she spoke up. "Well, of course he had us followed. Ran background checks, too."

Vicki looked up. "I hope you're so wrong."

"Your past that sordid?"

She nodded.

"I think Marge is right." Audrey leaned in. "See? I lied on my application and got to feeling bad about it. When I fessed up, he didn't act surprised at all—or mad either. I thought he would be so angry that he'd send me home."

In the same hushed tone, Holly asked, "What'd you lie about?"

"Being married before." She took a deep breath. "And having my ex-husband's name tattooed on my hind-end."

"You didn't have to lie about that. Shouldn't have answered at all. He didn't have one right to ask such a thing." Suppressed snickers went round the cavernous limo. Marge managed to swallow hers, but couldn't hide the grin. "Well, he didn't, but I could see how that would be a problem for you. So exactly what did he say when you told him?"

Audrey recounted the conversation in minute detail. In the end, Preston's reaction pleased Marge. A lesser man might have wanted to see the evidence. Once the cook finished her story, the others fell silent, leaving Marge alone with her thoughts.

If he were just choosing instead of planning out all these silly competitions, she'd feel a couple of points up on her chief competitor, boosted ahead by Audrey's lies. But no, she needed Lady Luck for a best friend. Lies obviously didn't bother W. G. Preston, and that wasn't right.

What awaited her that evening soon eclipsed any juggling for position or Preston's games. Stephanie had accepted her invitation for a fancy dinner, and her daughter would be like a pit bull to find out exactly what was going on in East Texas. But, in spite of everything, Marge looked forward to seeing her.

Soon the Dallas skyline appeared, and she took to planning her day. She had so many things she wanted to buy him, and knew the exact place to start. "Anyone want to share a cab to the Galleria?"

Vicki nodded. "Good idea. I'll go with you."

Marge looked around the car, but no one else showed much interest.

Holly spoke up. "Natalie and I decided to start at the West End, but we're not going until three when all the soaps are over. I mean we've got two days to shop." She shivered with giddiness. "Wish Charlotte was here to watch them with us. I probably won't even recognize anyone."

Audrey remained noncommittal.

At exactly one hour and twenty-two minutes after the car pulled off Preston's land and onto the farm-to-market, it eased into the circle drive of The Mansion on Turtle Creek. Marge had heard so many stories about the supposed ultimate in posh, but never in a million years dreamed she'd be spending two nights and experiencing The Mansion as a guest.

Sharing a cab to North Dallas ended Marge and Vicki's time together. The power walking young thing couldn't get away fast enough, but Marge didn't really mind. With so much serious shopping to do, she didn't want to have to keep up or be bogged down, either. By a little after three, she returned to her room loaded with sacks and bags.

Some quick calculating showed her she still had lots to spend as her purchases so far only added up to eight hundred forty-seven dollars and nineteen cents. Plus the hundred cash she'd gotten from the ATM, of which she still had sixty-three and some change.

She hated keeping track, but understood his need to know. Not that she agreed with him. In the end, though, it was his money, and she didn't really have any right to question the man or his methods. Except she still did whether it was her place or not. He shouldn't get to make all the rules just because he had so much money.

Oh dear. She rubbed her temples. He made her crazy. But could she live the rest of her life without him being a part of it? She tried to think what she'd do. What if this was her month to pack up and leave? How would she spend her remaining days? She didn't want to go back to her old life, but couldn't think of what else there would be without those early mornings with Preston, picnics with Preston, and Scrabble games with Preston. Yes, she was going crazy, like a teenaged girl fretting over her first puppy love.

A thought hit her out of the blue like a foul ball. What would Walter think of the man? Hmm. She hadn't thought of Walter lately, but he would like Preston. She frowned, somewhat uncomfortable over not thinking of him sooner, but her heart smiled. He'd be happy she found such a good man. Yeah, but finding and keeping were two different tricks. She might buy all the wrong things, or go to the wrong places. Oh dear. She propped up a pile of pillows and turned Oprah on.

When the time to meet Stephanie rolled around, the only thing for certain was that it had been a spell since breakfast, and Marge was hungry. She hoped her stubborn daughter wouldn't spoil their evening with all her questions.

Stephanie arrived right on time, and as promised, the maitre d' led them to their table at exactly seven-forty-five. Once seated, her only daughter scanned the menu. "Mother, please. How can you afford this? These prices are ridiculous." She looked around the room. "And you're staying at this hotel?"

"Don't worry about it. I have an expense account."

Stephanie shook her head. "Doesn't make sense, Mother. It's totally bizarre that you can't come home to visit, or that we can't even pay for a room and come to see you at this supposed bed and breakfast you're supposedly working at. When did a B&B ever not rent rooms?"

"The rooms have all been full."

"Oh, yeah, right. Then all of the sudden, you're staying at The Mansion and want to treat me to dinner. Totally bizarre."

"That isn't the right word, Stephie. Do you have to be so dramatic? Unusual maybe, but certainly not bizarre."

The girl started to retort, but the waiter arrived. Once she ordered, Marge held her off by asking a string of questions about the kids and her son-in-law. She nursed the topic until the dinner salads arrived, but provided only a temporary reprieve from the inquiring mind that wanted to know.

Stephanie sipped her wine then pointed her finger. "Mama, I want you to come home with me tonight."

"Sorry, dear, I can't. I've got an incredibly busy day tomorrow."

"Doing what?"

"Seeing to my employer's business."

"Doing?" Stephanie waved her hand as if to coax an answer.

"Can't say."

"Why not?"

"I signed a piece of paper that promised I wouldn't. I gave my word, so end of discussion."

"No, it isn't. It can't be. This isn't you."

"Oh, Stephanie, don't spoil our time." Marge drained her wineglass then nodded toward the waiter. "And why do you say it isn't me?" As the man approached, Marge gestured. "Another, please."

"Mother, you need to come home—to stay. I don't like you being so far away and not knowing what's going on."

"Look, my darling daughter, who I love with all my heart." The waiter refilled their glasses then retired discreetly. "I'm not doing anything illegal or immoral. So don't be worrying about me. Hopefully someday I can tell you all about it, but I'm determined to see this through."

"But why, Mother?"

"Because I owe it to myself."

CHAPTER FIFTEEN

Journal entry—May 31ˢᵗ
  Justice delayed is justice denied. She who tried to win by the sword lost because she wanted to go clubbing in Deep Ellum

Five minutes after they left, he wanted the women back home. The house creaked and groaned in the silence. Too quiet. He called his old cleaning service and had them work their sparkle and shine, but that didn't alter his foul mood. That first day and the next, he did his best to put the ladies out of his mind. By noon Thursday, they would not be put off any longer. He retreated to his office for the only balm he'd found—his journal. It couldn't be seven-thirty soon enough.

However, until it was, he consoled himself with his remembrances. Too bad he'd made such a big deal about sending one home every month. He paid for six months of their time, should get to enjoy their company that long. But that wasn't the deal, and he prized his word too much to change the rules now.

He'd lost himself working on her pages when the sound of tires crushing gravel pulled him back to the moment. He hurried to the back patio and slipped into a chair before the limo pulled past the house. Wouldn't do for them to know how bad he missed them. Though if anyone proved observant, she could tell. The car stopped. He remained seated.

Vicki popped out first, toting two huge bags. So young and lovely and energetic. He liked it that she asked him to adopt her. She needed a daddy to show her some attention and teach her about men. In that arena, the girl seemed bound for trouble without intervention. She smiled on her way in then returned to join the others huddled at the back of the car. She looked his way.

"Thanks for the trip, Dub. I never knew shopping for someone else could be so much fun."

The driver slipped between Marge and Natalie and opened the trunk. The lid popped up like one on a pirate's chest with jewels overflowing, and the women dove in extracting their treasures. Preston strolled in that direction, and they hovered like hens keeping their chicks from the eye of the hawk. "Well now, should I have sent a bigger car?"

Audrey nodded as she wrestled one huge bag into the house. "Actually, maybe a U-haul."

He watched the frenzy a moment then made his way to the kitchen. The women migrated in, lugging their purchases. The trip to Dallas obviously met his every expectation. The ladies seemed renewed and excited—all smiles—and he liked making them happy. Especially since one of his little clutch wouldn't be so cheerful in a matter of minutes. He wished again there was another way, but put it out of his mind. After all, he still had all those surprises ahead.

A tablet and pencil waited on the table at each place. He found his chair, motioned for them to take their places, then pulled out the two pages of rules. "Okay, my dears. I'll see the loser afterwards in my office. Glad no one was late. Anyone go over the limit?" He looked to his left.

Vicki shook her head. "Not me."

He looked around the table, but got no responses. "Excellent, because if anyone had, she'd be packing about now." He cleared his throat. "Okay then, get ready to write. Who bought me underwear?"

Everyone grinned or giggled, and all but Vicki raised a hand or spoke up.

"Plus twenty points if it's all white. Minus twenty if it's colored—or the wrong size."

"What's the right size?"

He told them. Two of the five groaned.

"Well that's silly. Why would you do that?" Marge asked.

He leaned back and studied her a moment. He hadn't figured she'd be the one to question him, seeing how she didn't like his games anyway. Besides, she'd marked her scorecard with twenty points in her neat plus column. "Because I hate to take anything back, and everyone knew I said shop for me, but did anyone have the forethought to ask my sizes? No. So if you guessed right, you get points, otherwise it's a minus."

She didn't respond, which he took as an aggravated acceptance. He liked a woman willing to stand up to him, but who knew when to sit back down. Marge didn't let her spunk overrule her respect.

"Plus thirty points if you bought me anything wooden."

"Cool." Vicki scribbled on her paper.

"Awe, rats." Holly slapped the table. "I started to get you this wooden apple boxie thing, but you had wood on the first list. I figured you wouldn't repeat. Why did you?"

"I like wood. It's natural, beautiful, and lasts a long time." He raised his eyebrows. "Okay, plus forty if you bought me quality work clothes. Same thing on wrong sizes. I wear two-x shirts and forty-two/thirty-four pants. Add thirty points for leather work boots. Minus thirty if they're not size twelve."

Natalie smiled at Holly then each jotted down points.

"Anyone buy me a suit?"

"I did. It's pure silk." Audrey beamed.

He rattled the paper suddenly wishing he hadn't made it so many points. "Minus fifty."

She pushed back her chair. "Fifty? Why? It's you. You'll look so good in it."

"Where would I look good in it?"

She held out her hands. "Right here, right now. I'll go get it. Just try it on, and we'll all melt in your glow." She stood. "Tell you what. You try it on, let the women vote."

"I'd love to see you in a suit." Vicki pumped her eyebrows.

Marge reached for Audrey's hand and held it. "Me, too, Dub."

"Nice try, but it says right here minus fifty." He thumped the paper. "And that's that. I haven't left the place in five years and don't plan on going anywhere anytime soon. That's why I decided on this one. You all know that."

Audrey sank back into her chair. "But fifty points."

He would like nothing better than to take her up on the voting offer and wished she hadn't chosen a suit, but he'd put it down, so he couldn't change it now. "Let's move along." He refocused on his list. "Anyone get me a movie?"

Vicki nodded at Marge who blushed. They grinned like two kids about to bust with a secret. "Lady Bug did even better than that."

He faced Marge. "Oh, you did? Tell me what's even better."

"A forty-eight inch DVD-TV combination and fifty old movies they've converted to compact disk with comments from the director and stars." She shrugged. "At least those who are still alive. Or maybe they dug up old interviews."

"Really?" He studied her then remembered she'd been in his bedroom. "Excellent, seems like it should be worth more, but give yourself twenty points."

"Thank you."

"Anyone buy a game?"

Vicki spun around in her chair. "Can I double dip?"

"Like how?"

"Well, I already counted the chess set as being wood, does it count again as a game?"

"Well sure. Give yourself another twenty points."

He waited until she finished then checked the next item. "At first I had it limited to a leather belt, then I changed it to anything leather is good for twenty points."

"What about triple dipping?" Vicki leaned back with a smug expression plastered on her face.

"Double, triple, whatever."

"Good, cause the chess set has a hand tooled leather case."

"Count it."

"Did anyone buy me anything from a discount store?"

Holly raised her pointer finger and grimaced.

"Minus twenty. And here's the rest. Fiction books, plus twenty-five, non-fiction, plus ten. Magazines, minus thirty. Computer software, plus ten." He folded the paper. "Okay, ladies, that concludes the buying half."

Several talked at once.

"Wait, what about trees?" Natalie twisted the end of her ponytail. "I have a dozen fancy-dancy new strain of apple saplings being delivered ASAP. Do I get any points for those?"

Audrey bit her lip. "And what about art supplies? I bought you canvases, brushes, and oil paints in every color."

He held up his hands. "Sorry, art supplies wasn't on the list, but I like the thought, and yes, Natalie. Count thirty points for the trees since they've wood. Well, hey, Audrey, are the brushes wood? Count them.

"But we're not done. That's just the end of the buying part." He gave Audrey a little grimace. "Couldn't cover every

133

base, sorry, girl." With the first page back in his pocket, he spread the second sheet. "Who went to the West End?"

As though joined at the hips, Natalie and Holly spoke up. "We did."

"Together?"

Holly shook her head. "Well, we went together. Shared a cab, but we didn't stay together."

"What about Deep Ellum?"

Natalie nodded. "How'd you know? That's where me met back up later that night at this great club Holly knew about."

He shook the paper. "Sorry, being alone in the West End is minus thirty points and another forty for going to Deep Ellum by yourself." He looked at the other women. "Anyone else go to a bar or club alone?"

Vicki grimaced. "Hotel bar count?"

"Yes, ma'am."

She filled her lungs then poised her pen over her paper. "Minus thirty."

He waved his page. "Did anyone do anything stupid, like bungie-jumping, racecar driving, or going to a bowling alley?" Several smiled, but no one spoke up. "Good. Who visited friends or family?"

Marge nodded. "I had dinner with my daughter, then the next day, visited with my grandchildren at Old Town Park."

"Hey, that's not fair." Natalie pouted. "I don't have any friends or family in Dallas."

"Fine, did you call any friends or family?"

"Well, no."

"Enough said. Marge, plus sixty points."

"Do I count it once or twice?"

He glanced at the Polynesian beauty. "Twice." He refocused on the rules and found his place again. "Okay, going to a church or a museum is worth fifty, a movie twenty. Add an extra ten if it was an Indy." He pulled the other page out of his pocket and tossed them both on the table. "That's it. Anyone have any questions?"

"Yes, sir." Vicki picked up the top sheet. "Not that I went, but was bowling a good or bad thing?"

"Bad."

Natalie's expression could sour sweet milk. She could hardly look him in the eye. "Why was going to the West End and Deep Elm such a big minus?"

"Not a place I'd want my wife going alone."

For the next few minutes, the only sound was pencils scratching and paper rattling as everyone took turns looking over the rules. Finally, they finished.

"Marge, why don't you start?"

"Two hundred and thirty points. But I still don't like these competitions of yours."

He tipped his imaginary hat, then looked to Audrey.

She cut her eyes and spoke barely above a whisper. "One forty."

Holly raised her head. "You're safe." She arched her back a bit too much and bit her bottom lip. "Ninety."

Natalie melted into her seat looking much better. "A smooth even hundred. Sorry, Holly."

Vicki glanced to her left. "So am I, Holly. I've got a hundred and fifty."

CHAPTER SIXTEEN

Journal entry—May 31st

I would be surprised if there wasn't royalty in her family tree. What a lady.

After one knock, Holly peeked around the door. "Hey, Dub."

"Come on in." He stood and gestured toward the wingback. "Have a seat."

She slipped into the chair. "Don't feel bad, Dub. It's been fun. Really. Actually, I never figured I'd last this long."

He nodded, sat back down, then slid the two legal size pages toward her. "I'd like you to sign this. Take as long as you need to read it."

She scanned the top page, flipped it over, then inked her name on the second. "You don't have to worry about me. I understand your need for privacy."

"Good." He exchanged the pages for her check. "Hope this lessens the sting some."

She unfolded and kissed it, then smiled at him. "It's been great." She scooted to the edge of her chair. "Want some advice?"

"Sure."

"Don't let Audrey get away."

He laughed. "Sure tend to agree with you about that."

Holly stood. "Well, time to go pack. I'll be ready at seven.

Now, I don't want to sound uninterested, because I still am, but if you don't mind, I'd rather not have a goodbye kiss."

"I understand." He hurried to the door and opened it. "Keep in touch. I'll send you an invitation to the wedding."

She nodded and winked. "I'll be looking forward to it. See you."

He waited until she disappeared around the corner before he closed the door and returned to his journal. He found Holly's pages, made a few notations, then flipped back to the rules section.

Something dogged him about his plans for the next month, but his mind's finger couldn't quite grab it. For the longest, he let his mind wander hoping whatever bugged him would worm it's way to the front. It never did, so he gave up and went to bed.

By his second cup of coffee on the patio the next morning, he had it all figured out. Solving the mystery, purchasing an antique, joining the Pulpwood Queens, or winning the costume contest would buy a lady another month. The faint warning of displaced gravel at the front gate pulled him from his deliberations.

He waited a second to make sure it wasn't someone turning around, then strolled toward the circular drive as the crackling increased. He reached the corner of the house just as one of the sheriff's sedans rolled to a stop. Much to Preston's surprise, the man himself got out of the cruiser.

"Morning, James T." He held his out. "Want a cup?"

"Love one, W.G."

"Black with a dollop of vanilla ice cream?"

James T. smiled. "You bet, when I can get it."

In no time, Preston poured the sheriff a fresh cup of vanilla coffee, and his long-time friend headed toward a chair.

Once the man got his boots under the table, he shook his head. "Hate having to ask, but I've had a complaint filed and—" He waved as if it were nothing, then shook his head again.

Preston lowered himself to eye level. "Come on, now, spit it out. Can't be that bad."

The sheriff removed his hat and fondled the shape of the brim as he looked around the room. "You holding a middle-aged woman here against her will, W.G.? Well, more precisely, have you brainwashed this alleged lady into your new religious cult?" The words sounded rehearsed.

Preston tried not to smile but couldn't help it. "I've got a couple of ladies staying here who might fit that bill. Got a name?"

He nodded. "Marge Winters."

"She's here."

"Can I talk to her?"

Preston pointed toward the hall. "She's usually up by now, but I guess we can wake her if you want."

He placed his hat on the table. "No hurry, as long as the ice cream lasts."

Marge had heard the car but worked it into her dream. For forty winks or so, she watched the night vision, then sat up wide awake. Her ears strained to catch the faint melody of Preston's bass. Another man's tenor brought her to her feet. She peeked out her window. Hmm. A sheriff's car rested in the circle. It hadn't been a dream.

She threw on her housecoat and hurried to the kitchen. Preston sat elbow to elbow with a man dressed in a starched white western-cut shirt. A shiny silver star adorned his chest. She stopped at the doorway. Preston looked up. She loved the way he smiled at her.

"Morning, Marge. James T. here would like a word with you."

"With me?"

The lawman stood. "James T. Johns, ma'am, Van Zant County Sheriff. I'd be pleased if you'd allow me to ask you some questions." He pulled out the chair next to him. "Could I get you a cup of coffee first, ma'am?"

Preston jumped to his feet. "I'll get it. You ask away."

The sheriff sat in Marge's chair, so she slid into Audrey's. It didn't fit. "What's this about, Mr. Johns?"

"Please, call me James T. Now, I understand you're in this here ol' codger's employment. How long's that been, ma'am?"

"Three months."

"You like it here?"

"Certainly. What's not to like?"

Preston returned with her coffee, set the mug in front of her, then took his seat. He wore a bemused smirk. She wished he'd share the joke.

"And have you been back home since you came, ma'am?"

She glanced at Preston who shrugged then looked back to the lawman. "Excuse me, Sheriff. I'd like to know what this is all about."

"I've had a report filed, and I'm trying to determine if there's anything to it."

"What kind of report?" She looked back to Preston. His smirk had grown into a full-blown grin. "And what about those feathers hanging out of your mouth? What are you so happy about?"

"You."

"Me? What about me?" Her cheeks warmed. "Will someone please tell me what's going on?"

James T. waved her off and stood. "Oh, nothing to worry about, ma'am. W.G. here can fill you in. I oughta be getting on back to work." He picked up his white Stetson.

Preston stood. "We'll walk you out." He stopped at Marge's chair, helped her to her feet, then didn't let go of her hand as they walked outside. Tingling sparks raced from the tips of her fingers to her heart. Once on the patio, she remembered to breathe and not to gasp.

The sheriff slipped into his car then rolled down the window. "Almost forgot, W.G., there's a reporter type asking around town for directions out here."

"That so?"

"Yeah, but from what I hear, everyone's giving her bad instructions." He smiled. "Wouldn't do for the second richest man in Van Zant County to be entertaining any unwanted visitors."

Preston formed his finger into a gun then shot the sheriff. "Yeah, but my money's more liquid than Henry's."

"That it is." He tipped his hat again at Marge, rolled up his window, and pulled away.

She held her peace until he rounded the corner. "Now, what was that all about?"

"Stephanie, I'm guessing, is claiming that I've brainwashed you into my new religious cult."

"No."

"If not your daughter, then who?"

"But I just saw her in Dallas."

He nodded toward the house. "Doesn't matter. What I like is the way you handled James T."

From the heat, she knew her cheeks must be flame red, but hopefully the pre-dawn darkness hid the crimson shade. "I appreciate that." She stopped short of the light and grinned at him, but didn't let go of his hand. "So are you really the second richest man in Van Zant County?"

He turned around framed in the pale glow of the kitchen

light. "Actually, I'm the richest."

"Oh? You are?"

He nodded. "Yeah. May not have Gates' kind of money, but I could buy several small countries."

"I always wanted a small country." She nodded over her shoulder. "Wait a minute here. Then why did—?"

"Old joke. James T. and I've been knowing each other since second grade." He pulled her gently into the light. "Forget about that. We need to figure out how to handle this reporter. But first, let's get a refill." He let loose her hand then took her mug. "Be right back."

She loved the way he performed small courtesies for her— and the others. Well, truth be known, she really didn't like it when he paid the other ladies any attention at all, but what right did she have not to like it? So she tried her hardest not to be resentful, especially over him calling Vicki darling all the time.

And forget all the ladies, how could Marge know for certain if she really cared for him or was just wanting to win the game? The question drove her crazy. He returned with the coffee before she could decide, and suddenly, it no longer mattered.

CHAPTER SEVENTEEN

Journal entry—May 31st
   In principle, I like the idea of the free press, but sure wish having money didn't put you in the public domain.

Preston and Marge looked at the reporter problem like two kids poking a horned toad with a stick. Before the two bloodied the thing, Audrey joined them, got caught up, then pulled out her own prod. A few minutes later, Natalie slid into her seat with a fresh cup of coffee, heard enough to figure out the gist of it, and took a so-what attitude. Not until Vicki joined the assembly did a possible solution present itself.

Marge raised an eyebrow then shook her head. "Might work, but why take the chance?"

Vicki slung one hand skyward. "What if this woman doesn't give up? I still say we've got to give her something."

"Hold it." Preston eased her forearm back to the table. "Nowhere is it written that we have to talk to the press." He smiled even though he didn't relish seeing his name or that ugly file photo they'd use splashed across the front page of the paper. Never mind the TV or internet. "Without confirmation, no one's going to print anything if they're worth their salt."

Natalie twirled the end of her ponytail and yawned. "They may already have it. Surely you've heard that old cliché hell hath no fury . . ."

142

Her words ended, but he knew where she was going. "I don't think it was Charlotte." He smiled. "And, please, don't call me Shirley."

A puzzled look came over Natalie. She had to think a minute, but slapped at him when she finally got it.

He looked at Marge who lifted her shoulders once. "Couldn't have been Dot."

Vicki stood and stretched before making her way to the fridge. "Well, it couldn't be Holly. She just left." She refilled her stemmed goblet with orange juice.

"What about Virginia?" He glanced at Audrey, and she looked away. Why did she have such a vendetta against Virginia?

"No, don't think so. I talked with her last week, and she didn't sound like someone who'd been talking to a reporter."

The name of each lady who'd left their clutch got trotted around the kitchen table several laps before Marge jumped off the merry-go-round. "But don't you all see that it doesn't have to be one of them at all?"

Vicki took the bait. "Then who?"

She stared at the table top a minute then looked around the table and grimaced. "My daughter."

"Why would you think that? Did she say something when you had dinner with her?"

"No, but she went to the law and even filled out a complaint. She's headstrong and doesn't like not knowing what's going on out here."

Preston sat back while Marge told about James T.'s early morning visit then lost interest as the ladies worked this new angle. He'd already made up his mind. He liked Vicki's idea, and it didn't really matter who had tipped the press. The reporter needed handling.

He stood. "Okay, enough of this. I've got a new topic."

The women all stopped talking mid-sentence. "Four weeks from last Saturday night is the Mid-Summer Night's Literary Ball put on by the Friends of the Carnegie Library in Jefferson." He smiled. "Later today, another thousand dollars of credit will be added to your cards. Before the sun goes down, a nice young man who looks twelve but is really nine, will install your new computers so you can shop the net. I suggest you get to work on your ball gowns, ladies. You'll go as your favorite fictional character."

"So this is our new contest?" The fire in Marge's eyes could have fried his soul crisp had he been younger or less worldly, but it only hurt his heart a little. So feisty. Maybe someday, she'd trust him more.

"Sort of. But in this scenario, everyone can win. If they do, no one goes home."

Vicki tugged on his sleeve. "So tell us. Tell us. How do we win?"

"Always the questions." He looked to the other ladies. "Make yourself—and I stress make, no ready-made designs allowed—the best, most outstanding costume at the ball. There will be a contest with a couple of categories. And that's all you need to know for now."

Even so, for the next ten or fifteen minutes, he fielded questions, but other than confirming it was the Jefferson in East Texas—the quaint town of antiquing fame with a bed and breakfast on almost every corner—he didn't divulge any new information. Finally, he tired of their feminine chatter, snatched Vicki by the wrist, and retreated to his office.

He deposited her in the guest wingback then took his own seat. "So you think you can pull off the whole deal without the reporter catching on?"

"Do you really want to know?"

He leaned back. "Your past is colorful, but I don't recall any confidence work."

"True, but fooling folks is what I do best." She tried to smile but didn't quite manage it and ended up looking girlish. "Even if I couldn't fool you."

He liked it. Brought out the daddy in him, or was it the sugar-daddy? Could he help it if he loved buying the ladies things or rather letting them shop until they dropped? Isn't that what females loved to do? "Okay, then get to it. Go tell Jorje to give you the keys to the truck."

She stood. "Cool, and what do you want me to find out exactly?"

Marge had stationed herself in the far corner of the patio and pretended to read a book, but in reality, she watched for Vicki to come out of Preston's office. Audrey sat across the ornate wrought iron table and read a cookbook as though it was a novel.

"How long's it been?"

She looked up. "How long has what been?"

Marge leaned toward her, but didn't take her eyes off Preston's door. "Vicki. How long has she been in there with him?"

Audrey glanced at her watch. "Twelve minutes max."

The door opened and the young beauty moved through the odd little entry then disappeared toward her room.

"See? You didn't have anything to worry about."

"Of course I do. You've seen it. The way she follows him around like she's his new puppy or something."

Audrey marked her place, closed her book, and sat it on the table. "Big deal. So she's his gofer. What counts is how he looks at her, and he doesn't look at her—or me, or Natalie, either—the way he looks at you."

Even though Marge loved what her friend said, she didn't believe it. If he really cared for her, he wouldn't risk losing her with his silly games. "Nice of you to say, but I don't think so. I can't see it."

"You're blind as a bat, worse than blind. Why even a blind man could see he's smitten."

"Then why does he spend so much time with Vicki?"

Audrey made an exasperated face and shook her head. "So? He still talks to Virginia on the phone, but he doesn't love her, either."

"You don't know that."

"I know he doesn't love me." She pouted. "As much as I'd like for him to, he just doesn't." She wiggled her eyebrows and lowered her voice as though she didn't want anyone else to hear. "I do think he loves my chicken cordon bleu, though."

"You'd marry him if he asked."

"So? What that's got to do with anything?"

"Well, you don't think Vicki would, too? And you know good and well Natalie or Virginia would, so you can't say he loves me. Maybe he's just in love with the idea of having a wife again. So, it's not love you see in his eyes when he looks at me. Can't be. We don't even really know each other."

Audrey laughed. "Now didn't that tirade make a lot of sense? Of course he knows you. How many times does he have to ask you to inspect his apples before it sinks in he's got a thing for you?"

Marge waved her off. "Don't give me that. We're still playing his stupid games, aren't we? I could lose in Jefferson, and don't you think for one minute he wouldn't want to see me in his office for his exit speech and to sign his silly legal documents."

"I know, I know. But a costume ball. Doesn't it just sound

like so much fun? Who are you going as?"

"I don't know. Haven't given it much thought yet." Marge leaned back in her chair. In spite of herself, she couldn't prevent herself from being excited about what Audrey had said and the ball, too. She wanted to believe with all her heart, but she couldn't take any chances in Jefferson. She had to think of someone really special.

Neither had Vicki decided who she would be though she thought about going as Dick Tracy since comic books and western novels were about as literary as she got. A long yellow rain coat and yellow fedora would make a great costume.

She noticed Marge and Audrey sitting on the patio coming out of Preston's office, then again as she sped by on her way to the warehouse, but didn't really pay any attention. Protecting Preston consumed her. And he liked her idea. Now she had to make it work. At that moment, she wanted an 'at-a-girl' from him more than anything.

It took her exactly eighteen minutes to trot to the warehouse, explain to Jorje what was afoot, then speed off the property. In another eighteen, she sat in James T.'s office asking the man himself a favor in Preston's name.

"Not a problem, Miss Vicki. W.G. already called. The deputies tell me she's in her room at the Travel Lodge. Number Twenty-four." The sheriff rotated a site map to face her. A red arrow pinpointed the reporter's room. "Let me know if there's anything else I can do." He scooted it toward her. "You can take that."

She studied the piece of paper a second, found north, then recalled the one-story, flat-roofed, fifties-style motel that sat next to the gas station where the taxi had stopped that first day.

"Got it. Thanks."

She grabbed the paper, folded it twice then stuck it in her jeans' pocket. From the office to the truck, her heart rate quickened with each step. By the time she reached the motel, her cheeks burned, but she made herself focus.

If she was really doing what she pretended to do, then it would only be normal for her to be shook up. The thought calmed her some, but she decided she'd better act nervous. No. Forget nervous. She'd never practiced nervous. Sound reasoning looped back on her. She filled her lungs, blanked her mind, then tapped on the woman's door.

"Yeah. Be right there." Footsteps rattled the glass in the picture window. The door popped open a chain length's worth. "You the pizza girl?"

Vicki shook her head. "No. I understand you're interested in Winston Grant Preston."

The door slammed shut. The chain clattered on the inside. In point three seconds or better, a woman stood in the open door inviting Vicki's entrance with a grand wave of her arm.

She stepped inside then eased the door closed, but kept her hand on the knob. "You are the reporter who's been asking questions around town, right?"

The woman stuck out her hand. "Susie Waters. Guess I'd be the one."

Vicki threw her a nod, but ignored the hand offered. "I don't take checks. I want cash. Nothing larger than a fifty. When can you have the money?"

CHAPTER EIGHTEEN

Journal entry—June 2nd

> *Dick Tracy only wished he had as much guts. Oh, to have been a fly on the wall.*

"Excuse me?"

Vicki rubbed her thumb over her fingers. "Money? You know, show me the dough and all that."

"What are you talking about, Miss—Miss—"

"No need." Vicki tilted her head and raised an eyebrow. "So are you paying for information or not? I haven't got all day." She moved the curtain an inch, peeked out, then turned back and stared at the woman.

Waters retrieved the remote and muted the TV. "Look. I only need directions to his ranch." She smiled. "I've already got the angle. Just need a few minutes of his time."

"Not a chance."

"Why not?"

Vicki glanced out the curtain again. "No one who knows will tell, and even if you stumbled onto Preston's place, you couldn't get to the man."

"Miss—" Waters motioned for Vicki to help her.

Vicki smirked a 'no-thank-you.'

The reporter flipped her a catty 'whatever' smile. "So he's still in seclusion?"

"Afraid so." Again, she rubbed her thumb over her fingers. "So back to little ol' me, that is, if you want answers to your questions."

Waters threw her hands up and retreated a step. "Easy now, I can't afford to pay. Something maybe, but not much."

"How much?"

The reporter heaved a sigh then tapped her finger across her lips obviously thinking. "I'd have to talk with the editor. I'm doing this piece on speculation almost. Friend of a friend type deal." She ran her fingers through her hair from the front then rubbed the back of her head. "Look, I think maybe I can get a couple of hundred if you know what I'm after."

"No way would I betray my employer for a couple of hundred dollars. What are you? Crazy?"

"So—you work for him. You're not betraying anyone."

"Right. Me just being here would be seen as an act of disloyalty."

"No, not the man I've been reading about. Nancy said he was a big old teddy bear."

"Okay, you heard it from the dead wife herself." She turned the doorknob. "Guess you don't need me."

"Wait a minute."

"I want five hundred minimum."

"But I haven't got that much on me."

Vicki cracked the door. "See you around."

"Wait, I can get it."

She eased the door back closed. "How soon?"

"Where's the nearest ATM?"

Vicki slipped into the imitation leather desk chair next to the door. "Don't use the things myself, but I seemed to remember seeing one across the street."

Waters grabbed her purse then stopped. "Don't go away."

"I'll be here." Vicki waited to fill her lungs until the reporter slipped out. She'd done it. She held out her hands. "Solid as a rock," she said aloud then immediately chastised herself for being too cocky. Some gloating could be expected, but her ruse dictated she walk a fine line.

Besides, something was missing. Either this gal played coy well or didn't know about the choose-a-wife game Preston played out at his Apple Orchard Bed and Breakfast. Except, was it really a game? She remembered telling everyone early on that he wasn't a Harvard type who had all this figured out.

After getting to know him, she'd choose Preston for her team over any egghead on about any topic. His knowledge and the way he thought fascinated her. Had he done all this knowing how she and the others would react? She let her mind sniff around the deep hole she dug for Winston Grant Preston.

"You that smart, Dub?" Before she could answer herself, the key turned, and the door opened. "Get the money?"

"Most of it. I only had three hundred left on my card, and I've got another fifty I can give you."

Vicki stood. "Sorry, no way. If what I know isn't worth five hundred then—" She stepped toward the door.

"Wait."

"For what?"

"Answer one question. Were you working there when Nancy was still alive?"

"No." Vicki wished she'd said yes.

"Then I don't know if you can help me."

"Fine. I'm outta here."

The reporter grabbed her arm. "Please, can't we talk?"

Vicki stared at the woman's hand until she released it. "Look if I can't help you, and you don't have any money, we're done."

"You're right, but maybe one question? I'll give you fifty

for your trouble if you answer just one question."

Vicki pretended to consider the offer. She definitely wanted to hear the question. Maybe she should ask for more money, didn't want to seem too cheap. "I already answered one question, so I'll take the fifty. What else you want to know? Keep in mind the answer may or may not cost you more."

Waters pulled out a wad of money, forked over fifty, then counted out another. "How did Nancy Preston die?"

Vicki took the money. "Car wreck. A drunk hit her head-on."

"How come that's not in any of the newspaper stories?"

"Beats me, but that's two questions." She held out her hand, palm up.

"So you know a lot about her?"

She curled her fingers back and forth. "Yes, and that's three now."

"Come on give me a break. I've got another two fifty. Can't we visit a while for that?"

Vicki eyeballed the woman a second. She didn't seem like a muckraker. "You said earlier you had an angle. What is it?"

Waters shrugged. "A man—not any man mind you, but one of the richest men in Texas—is still grieving over his dead wife after five years. If I can find out about the real Nancy Preston, then I'll have a piece worthy of the *Sunday Dallas Morning News*."

Vicki nodded toward her hand. Waters greased her palm. "What do you want to know?"

For the next hour, Vicki answered the reporter's questions to the best of her recollection. So, in essence, she was being paid for her research. Nice how things work themselves out. Once they started covering the same ground twice, Vicki extracted herself with a promise to call if she thought of anything else.

On her return to the B&B, it took longer to tell Preston and the other ladies about the encounter than her little snoop-dog escapade actually took. When she finished, no one spoke. Vicki couldn't get a feel for Preston's reaction, couldn't read him.

Before he said anything or indicated how he planned on handling Miss Waters, Marge spoke up. "Well, Dub, I for one think it's a wonderful idea." She smiled. "I think you should have Vicki bring her out so you can tell her about Nancy yourself."

He leaned back and looked to the ceiling. "I don't know. What if it's all a ruse?"

Vicki waved the notion off. "I don't think so, but can't we check her out?"

Preston nodded. "As we speak."

Marge touched his forearm. "So there you go. If her story's true, then let her have the lowdown directly from you, so it'll be accurate."

"There's merit to what you're saying, but it's never been my policy to talk with the press. I'll think about it." He nodded at Vicki. "Thanks."

"Anytime, Dub."

"So, anyway, how are your costumes coming, ladies?"

He listened to the three tell him about their appointment with the kid genius who got them wired up and ready to surf, but past that, hadn't done much yet. What he condensed to a paragraph took the women over thirty minutes to relate. He shook his head. The rabbits those ladies did chase, but he enjoyed the hunt greatly.

Their dainty words fell easy on his ears and let most of his mind concentrate on the reporter. In the end, he decided to invite her to lunch. When he stood, the ladies all stopped talking leaving a silence in the place of chatter. He loved it, though he knew he should be more polite.

"Marge, could I have a word with you?" He held out his hand.

"Certainly."

He pulled her to her feet then guided her toward the patio. The cool, overcast night reminded him of fall, his favorite season, even if it was June. He loved everything about Texas except its blasted summer heat, and he didn't look forward to the blistering months ahead. No words passed until she stopped at the goldfish pond.

"Why do you think I should talk with this reporter?"

"So that the world, or at least our corner of Texas, can better know the woman you loved so much. She must have been a special lady."

He nodded then motioned toward the stone bench. She took his hand, and he helped her sit down before slipping in beside her. "Maybe you're right."

"Never hurts to have a friend at the paper, either."

"Oh, I could buy the paper if I wanted. Bought a PR firm once so they could work for me."

"What'd you do with it?"

He scooted around. "You smell good." He remembered the fragrance she had worn the first day he met her, but this was different. "What is it?"

"Elizabeth Taylor's Passion. I liked it."

"Well, I love it." He drifted closer, closed his eyes, and inhaled deeply. "It's new."

"Got it on the Dallas trip. Used my own money by the way."

He opened his eyes and leaned back. "How come I didn't smell it inside?"

She smiled. "Maybe I didn't want you to until we were alone."

"Good answer." He closed his eyes again and sniffed his way to her neck. His lips stopped a fraction of an inch short of where he wanted. For just a second, he lingered there then pulled back. "You know?" He stood. "Sometimes I think, oh no, what if Nancy finds out?"

Marge hugged herself as though winter had ousted summer's ill-tempered heat. "I don't know what to tell you, Dub. Maybe talking to this reporter will help you sort things out."

"What would your Walter think of me?"

She laughed. "I've thought about that. He'd like you. Probably want to punch your lights out for making time with his girl." She smoothed her dress. "But overall, I think he'd approve. You're an honorable man, and he respected a man who kept his word."

He nodded a thank you. "So you think I should talk with Miss Waters?"

"I would if she wanted to profile Walter."

He extended his hand and pulled her to her feet. "Okay. If she checks out." He stepped into her space and breathed her presence. "I almost kissed you a minute ago."

She eased closer until the length of her forearms rested against his. "I know."

He released her hands then traced her hairline with a finger. "Do we care there's probably three pair of eyeballs fixed on us?"

She smiled. "Four, counting Jorje."

"That Mexican's always sneaking up on me, and I never can catch him."

She chuckled. "Well, are you going to kiss me—or not?"

He tilted his head and pressed his lips against hers. Their softness exceeded his expectations. He wanted to devour her, eat her alive, but instead, eased back and filled his lungs with her. He held her shoulders, moved her slightly back, and focused on her image. For a second, he let his eyes feast on her beauty then burned the memory into the gallery of his heart.

She opened her eyes.

"You taste better than you smell, and you smell just marvelous."

"Thank you."

Without taking his eyes off her, he motioned with his right hand. Within seconds, Jorje stood beside him. "What is it, *amigo?*"

"Miss Waters. She checked out, Boss. I talked with her editor and the editor-in-chief."

"Good. Go tell Vicki to come here." He winked at Marge then faced the house.

She snuggled in next to him. "Does this change anything?"

He looked at her. "You talking about Jefferson?"

She nodded once.

"No."

She stepped away, glared until Vicki neared, then marched into the house.

He watched her disappear—why did she have to act like that—before facing the younger woman. "Vicki, darlin'." He spoke loud enough for Marge to hear. She broke step, but didn't turn around. "Go invite Miss Waters to lunch tomorrow, if you don't mind."

CHAPTER NINETEEN

Journal entry—May 31st
  Never should have kissed her.

Marge slammed her door shut then headed straight for her bed where she knelt and pulled out her suitcase. There might not be a jet plane out front, but she'd bet she could get a taxi. Either way, she was leaving. Another night under his roof would be one too many.

She hated him, hated it that he put more stock in his stupid game than her. That's what it amounted to. Well, she'd make it easier for him to narrow his choice down to one. Tears welled, but she blinked them away. No crying over him, either. She flipped the case open, then stared at it.

What was she doing?

Her nose tingled, and her sinuses filled. An arrow stabbed her heart. She didn't want to leave. She wanted to kiss him again, be with him and share her life. Why did he have to charge so high a price? What life would they have together based on luck instead of love? And was she ready to admit love on her part—much less dare to imagine it on his?

As if to answer her own question, a future flashed before her mind's eye. Two old people who looked somewhat like them hovered over a felt covered table cutting high card to see who walked the dog.

Humph. Preston wouldn't even have a dog. Too needy. Soon as she got home, she would buy her a puppy with some of his money! For a moment, she stared at the white-haired couple then shook the image away and settled on leaving. Forget wrinkles and folding.

The bag soon overflowed with all her belongings. She had much more than when she came. She hadn't realized. After careful poking and much tucking, she sat on top of the suitcase, latched the buckles, then set it by the door. She'd call Stephanie first. That would help her keep her resolve. No, before she called Stephanie, she'd tell him goodbye. It was the least she could do.

After Marge stomped off to her room, Preston retreated to his orchard. Black clouds hid any trace of blue sky. In the near distance, lightning streaked to the earth. Just what he needed. He'd about worked off her searing glare when she came walking up the road. He chopped a couple more weeds then threw the hoe over his shoulder and headed toward her. He met her at the fence.

He smiled. "You know, the Greeks only wanted to know one thing about a man after his death. Did he have passion?"

She pursed her lips. Her eyes glistened with unshed tears. "What's that got to do with anything?"

"No one who knows you can say you're not passionate."

"Whatever. I just came to tell you goodbye."

He stared into her eyes. She didn't look away, and nary a tear fell. "Please don't."

"No, you please don't. Don't ask me to stay. I can't stand it another day. What if I lose?"

"But leaving doesn't make sense."

"Yes, it does." She backed away a step. "I'm sorry, Dub, but I'm through with the game. I'm going."

He shook his head. "Yeah, to Jefferson. I don't think anyone will lose this month."

"You can't say that. You've got rules, and if I lose, then you'll send me home because I'm not lucky. I never have been. Everything I ever had was because I worked hard for it. Even Walter."

He dropped the hoe and jumped the fence. He wasn't sure who was more surprised. "Please, don't go. You were so excited about the ball. I saw it in your eyes this afternoon. Besides, I want to see you all dressed up in your costume."

She backed another step. "Don't ask."

He matched her step. "You know you want to stay."

She looked away for several beats of his heart. "I'll think about it."

"Good." He nodded toward the house. "I bet Vicki's back. Come on. We need to word the confidentiality agreement, fax it to legal, and plan out tomorrow's lunch with this reporter. After all, you're the one responsible for her invite." He resisted the urge to slip his hand into hers.

First, the fax to legal got hashed out—Marge added the most—then the conspirators spent another half-hour working on the menu. At the last item, orange sherbet, he nodded toward Audrey. "You mind serving, or should Jorje ask one of his cousins?"

"No, I can serve, but then what? Should I leave?"

"No, no. Stay and eat with us, of course."

"Okay."

He faced Vicki. "What's your story?"

"I'm your faithful gofer."

"You told her that?"

"Well, no, not in those words."

"She didn't ask?"

"Not really. I told her that I told you she was my cousin,

and that I talked you into letting her ask a few questions about Nancy."

"So are you eating?"

"Sure, wouldn't miss it."

He faced Natalie. "What do you think?"

"I don't if I can help it. If it's okay with you, I'll be the one staying in my room."

"That works." He turned to Marge. "You in or out?"

"I'll help Audrey serve then be a fly on the wall."

"Take good notes."

She smiled. It warmed his heart that she couldn't stay mad at him long. "Okay. Don't you ladies need to do some net surfing and costume designing before supper?"

For the rest of that day and half the night, he recalled pertinent information he wanted folks to know about Nancy, even dreamed about her, which was rare these days. By the following noon, he figured he'd relived most of her life. He met the pickup in the drive and opened the door for his guest.

"Welcome to the Apple Orchard Bed and Breakfast, Miss Waters."

She stuck out her hand. "Thank you so much, Mr. Preston."

"Call me W.G."

"I'd be honored, and please, call me Susie."

He gestured toward the house. "Lunch is almost ready." Once she passed, he winked at Vicki.

She winked back, handed him the signed agreement on the way by, then caught up with the reporter. "See this great old hardwood floor in here?" Vicki pointed toward the hall. "Came from a skating rink in Louisiana, but not just any skating rink, the one that Nancy skated on as a little girl."

While his newest gofer-girl toured the reporter, Preston eased into the kitchen. Soon enough, the pair returned, and

160

Susie sat in Marge's chair picking at her food between questions. By sherbet time, he figured she must be done since she'd covered everything. The reporter leaned in close. "What about the guy who caused the wreck?"

"What about him?"

"I could never find any reference to his name, much less a trial or sentencing. Do you know where he is, what happened to him?"

Preston leaned back and studied her a second. She didn't flinch. "Living in Dallas, last I heard."

"And his name?"

"Oh, I guess that doesn't need to be mentioned. He's a good kid."

"A good kid who caused your wife's death then didn't even do any time?"

He looked over her head a couple more seconds. "No, not a day."

She clipped her pen to her pad. "I'm sorry. I shouldn't have—If that's an area you'd rather not talk about."

He shook his head. "No, needs telling. Nancy made me promise that I'd help the young man who hit her, never mind he was driving drunk."

"Oh, I see. Wow. Your wife certainly had a forgiving heart, but I bet that was hard for you." She set her ballpoint to the paper again with her shorthand notes. "So he got off?"

"Not completely. My attorney recommended mandatory rehab with continued testing. The boy's in college now, and from what his pastor says, he's truly remorseful about the wreck."

"Could I have his name for my records?"

"Can't see a need."

Waters started to say something else, but Preston silenced her with his eyes. "Okay then, Miss Waters." He stood and extended his hand. "Been a pleasure. Your cuz'll take you back."

Vicki took the hint and eased the reporter out of her chair. "Did I tell you about the apples Mr. Preston grows here?"

Waters gathered her things, thanked the man again, then followed her make-believe cousin out the front door while hearing all about dwarf apple species. Vicki waited until she turned onto the farm-to-market road before broaching the subject of cash. "You got the rest of my money?"

The Barbara Walters-wannabe dug into her purse and pulled out a neatly folded wad of crisp bills. "Hope you know I ended up driving all the way to Dallas and back to get this for you."

"Hey, I earned it, didn't I? You got your interview."

"So what about this rumor I heard this morning."

"What's that?"

"One about you and the cook and that other lady hanging around. Hear tell you women are some sort of secret harem."

Vicki laughed then bit the inside of her left cheek. "To quote Eliza Doolittle, now wouldn't that be loverly?" She wiggled a hubba-hubba hoochey-coo. "If only, if only, if only."

When she got to the highway, Vicki strapped on her seat belt and motioned for her passenger to do the same.

Susie complied. "I mean, you have to admit, even if he is an old man, he's still got that animal magnetism, doesn't he? Don't you think he's just a hunk? Like Sean Connery. I don't think that man will ever get so old he won't be a looker."

"Actually, it's too bad, but I have to work for my pay-check." She choked back the image of Audrey and Marge laughing over that lie. "Audrey's the cook, and Marge is Mr. Preston's personal secretary."

"That's not what we're hearing."

Vicki shrugged. "We might hear a lot in a long day, but we best not be printing any lies now." She cut a sideways glance at Waters. "Besides, why would you be discussing Preston anyway? I hope you didn't forget—"

"Oh, get real. I know how to keep my mouth shut. I overheard a conversation at that little Mexican restaurant, Two Señoritas I think, out on I-20. Two old men in the booth behind me." She shifted toward her door and stared out the window.

"Yeah, well, you best be sending the story for his approval just like you agreed."

The reporter threw up her hands. "Why are you so suspicious all of a sudden? Number one, I wouldn't think of printing a rumor, and number two, I should have a rough draft for Mr. Preston in a week. Final by mid-June."

"Good."

Nothing else much worth remembering was said, and again Vicki spent more time in the telling of her trip than the whole ride actually took. When she finished, she pulled out the additional buckage from Waters and tossed it onto the table in front of her boss. "Twelve hundred and twenty."

He pushed it back. "Keep it. You earned it, darlin'."

"Why, thank you, Mister P." She gathered it without arguments then stuffed it in her back pocket. "Thank you very much."

Of course, she loved money, but the look of approval in his eyes and his soothing tone when he called her darlin' were worth more than the wad of bills pressing into her derriere. Could her heart handle the immense weight and not burst?

No matter what happened, she had to stay a part of his life. Around him, she acted different, and lately, she could even say she'd been proud to be herself. What a totally new concept. She'd never much really liked Victoria Truchard. Yes, somehow, she had to fix it so she got to stay at the Apple Orchard Bed and Breakfast.

In her room, she undressed and thought again about Susie's visit and what the woman said. In front of the full-length mirror on her closet door, she appraised herself as her hips swayed. Stepping out of her jeans, she grabbed a scarf that draped the lampshade. She pulled it slowly around her neck.

An idea struck her. She retrieved a coined necklace from her jewelry box and sat it on top her head with the coins hanging over her forehead. Now the image of being in his harem came into better focus, but she couldn't muster that sensual little spark she'd felt the first time she interviewed with him. What was going on, and what was wrong with her?

What more could she do to insure a place there with him for herself? How could she make this way of life a reality?

CHAPTER TWENTY

Journal entry—June 14th
  Hope it doesn't stir anything up, but I want to know.

Soon enough the days piled on top of each other, and the ladies stopped talking about the reporter. With only a week to go before Jefferson, Preston had all but forgotten Miss Waters' visit. Then Vicki came running up the lane from the house waving a large manila envelope. "It's here, Dub."

He met her at the fence. "What's here?"

"I'm assuming Nancy's story." She handed him the un-opened, oversized letter.

"Thanks." He rolled it then crammed it into his back pocket. "What's Audrey cooking tonight?"

"Not sure, but she's been at it all afternoon. I can tell you it's something that smells totally grand."

"Good. And how's your costume coming?"

"Perplexing." She leaned against the fence. "Actually, I'm making three, but I'm not sure which one has the best chance of winning."

"What are they?"

For the next ten minutes, he concentrated on listening to her discuss her costume ideas and what she liked and didn't like about each. He tried hard to pay attention, but a part of him couldn't wait to read the article. That part never convinced his feet to move, so he stayed put and listened to Vicki prattle.

"So, anyway, what do you think? Which one?"

"Beats me. I'm not a judge this year."

"So? You have been in the past."

"Yeah, one year Nancy gave them a big check to fix up the library."

"I looked it up on the Net. Read all about those libraries Carnegie built. It's a shame there's so few left."

"Anyway, the Friends of the Library rewarded us by inviting us as their special guests for the evening. They asked us to judge, so we did." He gazed off a minute then smiled. "Nancy sure cut up her heels that night. Wore me out. Took a week for my feet to recover from all that dancing."

"So what else are we going to be doing in Jefferson? How about giving a girl a heads-up here? You've got me laying totally awake at night thinking about this trip."

He waved her away. "Nope, no way. It'd be cheating to make you privy to more information than the others."

She wrinkled her nose then backed out of his reach. "You're an old meanie. That's what you are. Well, all I can say is it had better be fair, and I'll win. I couldn't stand you sending me home."

He nodded toward the house. "Sounds to me like any one of those costumes will get you another month. You don't have anything to worry about."

She nodded half-heartedly with a smirk. Blatant unbelief shone in her eyes, but she held back the sarcastic yeah, right. She stepped back toward the fence. "So, is this where you jumped over when Marge said she was going home?"

"No." He pointed a couple of posts down. "We were up there."

"Hurt yourself?"

166

He shook his head and chuckled. "No, and I don't know who was more surprised."

"So, do the rest of us get a look at the story before it's published?"

"Sure. I'll go in and read it right now." He nodded toward the gate. "Walk back with me. There's something I'd like for you to do."

"Absolutely, Dub. Anything."

Marge, who all this time had been working on her costume, knew nothing about Nancy's article arriving or that Vicki had conspired with Preston. She was having too much fun with her gown. Never in her life had she gone to a genuine ball. It would be so much fun. She could have finished a couple of days ago, but purposely slowed the process and relished each stitch, each pale glistening sequin.

Someone rapped on the door. "Hey, you decent?"

Marge gently spread her gown on the bed then threw a sheet over it. "Of course. Come on in."

Vicki flung it open and sauntered in. "Susie Waters finally sent her story for our approval."

"Excellent." Marge stood. "Where is it?"

"He's got it now. Said we could look at it after supper."

She sat back down. "What's Audrey cooking that smells so good?".

"Don't know, but I've got a question." She slipped into the rocker that faced the bed. "You are going to Jefferson, aren't you?"

"Yes, I'm going." Then added to herself—and afterward, I'm leaving. "Why do you ask?"

Vicki traipsed over to the bed, caught a bedpost just below the spindle, then pivoted on her heel. "Dub wanted to know. Said the way you two left it, you'd agreed to think about it."

She stopped hanging an arm's length from the post and looked Marge in the eye. "Guess he hoped you'd thought about it enough and wondered about your decision."

"Why didn't he just ask me himself?"

She laughed and swung again with abandon. "Maybe because we all secretly failed junior high, and we're having to relive this part over again so we can get it right."

"What else did he say?"

Vicki rocked forward. "Well, I told him about all three costumes I'm making, and he said any one of them would get me another month."

She could just hear him. Any one of them will get you another month, *darling*. Her jaw tensed. "I thought we decided not to tell each other who we were going to be?"

"I didn't think that meant him."

Agreeing calmed her. The two speculated for a while about the anticipated article from Miss Waters then both tried to guess the origin of that wonderful smell emanating from Audrey's kitchen.

Audrey's kitchen. That's about right. It would never be Marge's kitchen. Even if Lady Luck kicked her in the behind and she was the last remaining prospective-wife, it would still be Audrey's kitchen. Dub would always miss her cooking, always be comparing Marge's against it and finding her fare lacking. Another mark on the reasons-to-leave side of her mental debate sheet.

A few minutes before six, Vicki announced she'd better check and see who had KP. Alone again, Marge uncovered the simple but elegant dress and continued sewing sequins. The constant debate continued in her thoughts. Soon enough, her mind veered back to what she'd told herself.

She'd go and enjoy Jefferson, but before he had a chance to read his rules and send her home, she was leaving. She'd just wash him right out of her hair like Mitzi Gaynor in South Pacific and be as fine without him as she was before him.

Explicit directions to the B&B winged westward to Mesquite, compliments of the U.S. Post Office, as Stephanie had agreed to pick her up on Sunday evening. When an approximate departure time from Jefferson became known, she would call her daughter. She focused on the leaving and not the have-left. She had to.

The hall clock chimed its first strike, bringing Marge back to the present and dinner's aroma. Her stomach growled. She put away thoughts of the future and the hard times ahead then eased on toward the kitchen. Audrey and Vicki stood next to the oven. Natalie sat at the table thumbing through a magazine. All the ladies, but no gentleman.

"Where's Dub?"

Natalie threw her chin toward his office. "He's been holed up in there at least two hours."

"Anyone told him it was six?"

Audrey chuckled. "He's a big boy. Guess he knows what time it is."

Marge's face warmed as she stepped toward her chair, but she remembered what Preston was doing in his office and reversed directions. Short of his door, she paused. Deciding she really didn't have anything to lose—seeing as how only eight days and Jefferson separated her from going home—she tapped on it. No answer. She twisted the knob and stuck her head inside. So what if it was off limits? He could send her home, but she sensed he'd do no such thing. She sensed he needed her. And there he sat staring at the stack of papers on his desk.

"Dub? You okay?"

Nary a muscle moved as though he was a statue. She

slipped in. Just before she closed the door, he looked up.

"You okay?"

He nodded then wiped his cheeks. "Susie did a good job." His full bottom lip quivered slightly when he spoke. He pinched the bridge of his nose wringing the inside corners of his eyes at the same time, then cleared his throat. "There's only a couple of small changes that need to be made."

"Good, I'm glad." She wanted to run to him, wrap her arms around him and hold him, erase his hurt. Poor dear man. She stepped to the edge of his desk. "Maybe this is exactly what you needed."

He looked up, his blue eyes surrounded by dozens of blood red, tiny streaks of lightning. "How's that?"

"Well, this might be a good way to experience a little more closure. Paying tribute by letting the world know what a great lady your Nancy was."

Preston stood, pulled out a handkerchief from his hip pocket, then blew his nose. "You may be right, I'm finding you usually are. What say we go see what smells so good?"

He walked her to the door and waved her on before he retreated to his bath. Bending over the lavatory, he splashed his face, patted it dry, put drops in his eyes, then marched to supper. Maybe they'd saved him some.

A slow-baked, beer-basted ham was the culprit of Audrey's delectable scenting. That and the candied yams covered with pecans and marshmallows. Beyond wonderful, probably the best he'd ever tasted. And that's what all the ladies said, too. After he'd eaten enough to where he could slow down, he pointed at Audrey with his fork.

"We could make a fortune opening a restaurant and serving nothing but this meal."

She beamed. "I'd love it. Let's start tomorrow."

"If I wasn't already rich, I'd seriously consider it."

She laughed along with the other ladies, but he took note of the rejection in her eyes. "Besides, you're still too busy getting ready for Jefferson, aren't you?"

Vicki grabbed his arm. "Speaking of Jefferson, exactly when will we be leaving and getting back? Come on, Dub. Inquiring minds want to know."

"You, my dear," he patted her hand, "and the other ladies are leaving Friday morning."

"Why? I thought the ball wasn't until Saturday night."

He thought about it a second, then decided it didn't really matter if they knew ahead of time. "That's right, but you need to be there in plenty of time for the Mystery Dinner which is on Friday night."

Natalie smiled. "Oh fun. I've been to one of those before. It was great."

Preston grinned back. "Glad you approve." He faced Marge. "The Hale House is also where you'll be staying Friday and Saturday night." He swung his gaze to Audrey. "Figured you ladies might want to spend some time antiquing downtown, so I've increased all your card limits in case you see anything for the place." He looked to Vicki. "Saturday, on to the only beauty parlor slash bookstore in these United States, Beauty and the Book, where you'll get the works including lunch with the Pulpwood Queens and a few Texas authors." He fluffed imaginary tresses.

"A horse-drawn coach will arrive back at your B&B at seven forty-five to take you to the ball. It starts at exactly eight."

"And if I may ask, what's a Pulpwood Queen?"

He ignored her.

"Excuse me. Pulpwood Queen?" Vicki asked again, but this time with more volume.

"You'll see, darling. You'll see."

171

CHAPTER TWENTY-ONE

Journal entry—June 27th
   Had a little twinge, but it was more right than wrong.

Thursday afternoon rolled around as usual, and Vicki still hadn't decided which of the three characters she would be. With better than an hour before supper, she figured she needed help and found him sitting on the bench staring at the pond. Like she belonged, she slipped in next to him. "Hey, Dub."

He nodded, but didn't look her way, just stared at the fish.

"You real busy now?"

"Kinda."

"Want to talk about it?"

He leaned back and looked at her. "Not really."

"Is it me?"

He laughed. She loved the sound of his soothing bass voice, but especially when he laughed. "No, darling. I was thinking about something Marge said the other day."

She nodded, then nudged her hip into his. "How about helping me out."

"With what?"

"Who should I go as?"

His left shoulder ooched up a smidgen, as the corners of his mouth drooped a hair. "Beats me."

"How 'bout I model them, then you help me decide?"

172

"Sure, but I'm not a judge this year."

"I know that, you already said, but I'm about going crazy." She bumped his hip again. "So what did Marge say? You can tell me."

He reached under the bench, pulled out the can of fish food, and popped the top. "I know I can, but I need to keep my own counsel on this one." He leaned toward the pond and spread a few flakes on the water. "Go tell the other ladies I said you could be first, third, and fifth in the fashion show."

She patted his knee. "Thanks." She stood then snapped her fingers. "Hey, I looked up the Pulpwood Queens on the net. They are so totally fun. Never heard of such a book club, but I want one of those wild jackets—and a tiara, too, of course."

He waved her away. She hustled herself straight to Marge's room. The door stood open, and her friend sat at the computer. Vicki slid in then closed the door behind her. Marge turned around and smiled. "It doesn't get so stuffy with the door open, but then you're subject to all the riffraff coming in."

"Yeah, right. But I know what you mean. My room, too, since it's been so hot outside." She pulled the rocking chair over next to her older friend. "So what did you say to Dub?"

"When?"

"I don't know, but he's sitting out by the fish pond staring into space thinking about whatever it was. I asked him. He admitted it was something you said, but didn't want to talk about it because he wanted to keep his own counsel." Vicki threw her hands into the air. "So what profound thing did you say to him?"

"Beats me."

"You're no fun."

"Sorry." Marge grinned. "So, have you decided yet?"

173

"No, but Dub said I could model all three tonight. Then he'll tell me which one he likes best. Said I could go first, third, and fifth."

Marge nodded. "Why not?" She didn't think it sounded fair, but what did it matter? Since she wasn't playing his silly game anymore, she had no compulsion to see that all was right, fair, and just. "That's good. That way I'll get to see all three, too."

She'd go to Jefferson, have herself a grand time, then be done with him and his old apple viney orchard. She'd miss the girls, though, especially Vicki. Thinking about missing anyone else in the house was against her own set of rules.

Vicki jumped to her feet. "Well, better go lay everything out. Haven't done a quick change in years."

Marge glanced at the wall clock. "We're eating first, right?"

"Yeah, I think so," Vicki said over her shoulder as she headed for the door.

Marge tried to get Preston off her mind, but the young girl's bit of news wouldn't be denied. What had she said to him that made him sit and stare at the fish pond? She strolled toward the lone window in her room then peeked out. He still sat there. What would it hurt to go see? Maybe he'd tell her.

Forty-eight steps later she sat on the other end of the bench, careful not to touch him. "Vicki said you were out here."

He looked over. "She did, now, and what else did she say?"

"Something about me saying something that upset you."

"Didn't wait long to run to mother, huh?"

His voice sounded harder, not as melodious as usual. Marge made herself not react. Didn't matter that he saw Vicki as a child since she now enjoyed her ex-participantin-the-W.G.-Preston-prospective-wife-sweepstakes status. "Thought I might help, but if you'd rather be alone."

"No, no. Not at all." He glanced at his wrist, stood, then extended his hand. "Shall we walk? We've got an hour before supper."

She let him pull her to her feet then keep her hand in his. Didn't mean anything. Just like him kissing her didn't mean anything. The warmth that spread from his hand to her heart didn't mean anything, either, because she wasn't playing his game anymore. He'd have to find his good-luck girl somewhere else. Her eyes watered, and she fought to make them stop. He was so wonderful.

A few feet past the house, he gestured at an overgrown path she'd never taken. "Sometimes," he explained once the trail widened and she could walk beside him, "I can't remember what Nancy looked like."

Oh, dear. She looked at his handsome face. Poor man. "Well, don't let it worry you, Dub. It's natural. Truly. Perfectly normal, believe me. Happens to all of us."

"I know, but it still bothers me some."

She didn't say anything back. In a few steps, the path topped a small rise then veered off to the right. He stopped. A beautiful little clearing surrounded by trees beckoned just ahead. Water spilled over a collection of boulders into an acre pond. "How lovely."

He pointed to the right. "There's a bench over there."

For the longest she sat next to him and studied the ripples on the water. Eventually, he spoke.

"Over there," he pointed to the far side, "is where I was going to build Nancy a house." His arm flopped into his lap as though ashamed for pointing out the spot. "But—" He shrugged then faced her. "I haven't given legal the final go ahead on her story."

175

"But why? You said it only needed a couple of changes. I was under the impression it was a wonderful piece."

"It is, but it's not complete."

She didn't know what to say. "Guess it's your call, but what could be lacking?"

"Besides helping the boy who hit her, she asked for one more promise." He stood then held out his hand. She let him pull her up.

"So that's what you've been brooding over?"

"Pretty much." He rose and started back. "You know who Andrew Carnegie was?"

"A rich old man who appreciated good music and good books?" She followed. "I know there were libraries all over the country that he built and there's Carnegie Hall in New York, right?"

"Sums him up. History may credit him with accomplishing more than that with his money, but yes, he's the one."

"So what about him?"

"Nancy asked me to do what Carnegie did."

"Build libraries?"

"No. Give all my money away."

"But why?"

"Why not? I can't spend it all. It's not like I'd give the orchard away, and I make more off it than it takes to live. It's appealing to know there wouldn't be such a huge estate left for the in-laws to fight over. Besides, the government would get almost half of it. I'd sure rather give it away to worthy causes than to them." He moved a branch back and let her pass. "Think of it. It can make a difference for generations. I mean, it's not like I tried to get so rich. I haven't done a deal in years."

Marge stopped walking and toyed with Preston's words. The more she thought about them, the better she liked the idea. "That sounds wonderful." She leaned back and tried to look into his soul. "Are you going to?"

"I've been trying, but I'm running into the same problem as Carnegie himself. My income is greater than what I'm able to give away."

She stopped and studied him a moment. Was he teasing her? He didn't appear to be yanking her chain. "How can that be?"

He shrugged. "Take the church fund. I seeded it with a billion dollars and told the board of directors there's more where that came from." He flipped his right hand in the air like the world had gone mad. "Because it takes so much red tape and time, they've only given away two hundred million, but that doesn't even cover the interest the money made in the last five years."

She nodded. He continued on his plan to aid struggling churches then started comparing that fund to three other charitable foundations he had set up that experienced the same difficulties. The legal aspects intrigued Marge, but the zeros he tossed around threatened her non-calculator-brain with overload.

The house came into view, and he stopped talking. She loved listening to him even if she didn't understand it all. Could she live her life without hearing the sound of his voice? Should she reconsider her decision to leave? "What else can you do?"

"I've got so many lawyers working on this they ought to rename the firm after me, and they all say it has to be done this way. I don't know, it's rather frustrating."

"A nice frustration, I would imagine."

"Not really. I didn't set out to be rich. Enjoyed the wheeling and dealing for a while, but one day I realized I had more than enough. Forget spending it all. I can't even give it all away."

CHAPTER TWENTY-TWO

Journal entry—June 27th

Jorje called. Said he and the gang had everything wired.

Vicki scooted the eggplant parmesan around her plate. She was so ready for this fashion show to start. She nudged her shoe against his. He wiped his mouth then turned toward her.

"You're not eating much. You sick?"

"No, just past ready to get my promenade over so I can decide what to pack for Jefferson. We leave in the morning after breakfast, if I remember the itinerary."

He smiled. "Snow White sounds mighty sweet, but what if I like Cleo or Maid Marian as much?"

"Now, listen carefully. You will like one at least a tiny bit more." She nudged his foot again then added under her breath, "You better help me out on this one."

"Darling, you don't need any help. You'll be fine." He winked. "Trust me."

She wanted to believe him, but knew how much he valued his dear rules. And he already had a list drawn up, of that she was certain. "Of course, I trust you. It's those judges in Jefferson I don't even know, so pretend you're a judge this year, and tell me what you really think. Okay? Please?"

He half-nodded, winked again, then forked another bite. "Delicious as usual, Audrey."

178

"Thanks, Dub. You're an easy man to cook for."

Vicki glanced around to see if anyone had been paying attention. The other ladies pretended not to be eavesdropping on her conversation with the man, but even as she checked each one's face, she knew better. In the end, did it really matter all that much if they knew now? Surely by then everyone had already decided who they were going to be. She pushed her chair back and stood. "Shouldn't I be getting ready?"

"Any time, darling."

"Good. Want me to come on back when I'm ready?"

He smiled. "Sure."

She returned his smile then hurried to her room. Before the echo of the door closing died, she had her blouse off and her jeans unbuttoned. She froze at her bed. Suddenly the order she'd planned didn't seem right. She grabbed the costume she thought to wear second, held it up against herself, then twirled and studied the mirror. She'd wear it, especially since Preston mentioned it first.

Shortly after the youngest of Preston's ladies left, the others decided on their order of appearance and scampered off to don their costumes. While he waited, he pondered who they might've chosen to appear as. He already knew the three characters Vicki agonized over. Before he made any hard mental guesses, the sound of beauty sliding over hard wood brought him to the here and now. The vision with a red ribbon in her hair glided into the room. Her full yellow satin skirt floated across the floor like she rode on air. Vicki wasn't just dressed as Snow White, she *was* the beautiful princess of Disney fame.

She cupped her hands together beneath her chin and sang a high-pitched aria like Snow White sang to the forest critters in the movie. He stood and clapped. "Well done. This one sure has my vote."

"But you haven't even seen the others."

He spun his finger around. She obediently twirled in a loose circle. "Excellent."

"Then I shouldn't even try the others on?"

He shook his head. "I didn't say that."

She hurried to him, stretched up on her toes, then kissed his cheek. "Don't you dare send me home. No matter what."

"I don't think you have to worry about that, not with that costume."

She stepped back, beaming, and curtsied. With her arms in the air ready for him to step into, she smiled. "Care to dance?"

He waved her away. "Later. The others want to show off, too."

Her lips turned down into a little girl pout, but her eyes still twinkled. "Okay, but you're dancing with me sometime before the night's over. Promise?"

"If you want. Go on now. Marge is next."

As if it had been planned for weeks, the oldest lady strolled in sixty seconds after the youngest left. Marge couldn't have looked more beautiful, from the subtle sparkles on the pale green material that draped her head to the jeweled sandals on her feet, her costume was perfect, even if he wasn't sure exactly which Bible character she was. Her darker green shift hung loose from her shoulders. The gathering at her waist by the multi-colored sash modestly accentuated her breasts before the material fell in graceful folds to her ankles.

"Lovely. You look perfect."

She smiled. "I'm glad you think so. I've always admired Esther's story."

He searched the corners of his mind, then remembered

180

the tale from Sunday School about the lady who saved her people from being destroyed by pleasing the king. "Wasn't she a queen?"

She nodded. "Named in place of Queen Vashti who basically refused to come when the king called. Esther saved her people from annihilation."

"I remember now. Yes, I like that story, too. But she couldn't have been more beautiful than you are right now." He twirled his finger again, and she turned. "It's you." He stood and held out his hand. "May I have this dance?"

She nodded and met him halfway. He took her in his arms and waltzed around the kitchen. Shame he wasn't going to Jefferson. He'd love nothing better than dancing the night away with all the ladies. After the second trip, he eased to a stop, then held his hand out toward her chair. "Let's sit a while. I think Vicki's dying for me to see her second costume."

Marge slipped into her seat. "She'd have to go some distance to beat the first. Her Snow White outfit was stunning."

He took his chair. "I thought so myself."

Shortly, Vicki slithered in crowned by a coiled golden serpent. A copper tubing wound from just beneath her chin to lay in graceful rows on her chest and made her neck look long, her head held regally high. The shimmering, skin-tight dress dazzled him. She probably had on more make-up than she needed, but it sure transposed her to a queen with her eyes fixed on the future of the upper and lower Nile and all those whom she ruled.

"Wow. You look more like Cleopatra than Elizabeth Taylor ever thought about." Preston shook his head. "I take back my vote for Snow White. This has to be it."

She seemed to melt. "Are you sure you love this one better?" She looked to Marge. "What do you think, Lady Bug?"

Marge held her chin and shook her head. "Well, I thought Snow White was stunning, but this. You do look exquisite, dear."

He shrugged. "I don't know which is better, darling. They're both so good." Preston winked and shooed her out. "Be off to Nottingham. Audrey's next, then we'll see your merry maid."

A few minutes later, the cook marched through the door. For a second, he wasn't sure who she'd chosen. Her hair clung to her head in soft waves with a twenties look, but her outfit seemed pretty normal to him, except for the Peter Pan collar and red checkered pinafore. Then it hit him. An apron. He should've known instantly. "Well, well, Miss Crocker. Or may I call you Betty?"

She grinned. "Oh, definitely Betty to you, kind sir. I know she may not be a who's who in the literary world, but she's in a hundred books—or a thousand at least—and once I thought about it, there really wasn't another choice for me."

Marge laughed. "Oh, you were so right, Audrey. It's perfect!"

Preston jumped to his feet, hurried to her chair, and held it out for her. "When you're right, you're right, Queen Esther. It's great."

Audrey eased into the seat and leaned toward her friend. "So you really think it'll be all right? I got worried it was too stupid once I had everything ordered."

"Oh, no. It's very original. Did you see Vicki's first two?"

Audrey nodded. "Yes, no wonder she can't decide."

Preston took his seat. "She wants me to choose, but I don't know. Which is your favorite?"

"Oh, both looked great, but if you think about the characters, neither is really her."

Marge shook her head. "You think? I thought either fit her to a tee."

Before the debate could continue, the object of their discussion hurried into the room. The rustle of angel wings announced her arrival. Yards upon yards of powdery blue, sheer material hung from a pointed hat as though enveloping Maid Marian in a little bit of heaven. Vicki had done something to her hair—twice as much as normal haloed her face with dark ringlets.

She shielded her eyes with her hand, then looked around frantically. "Oh Robin, my love. Where are you? Has anyone seen my Robin?" She hung her hand from her forehead. "Off to rob the rich so the poor may have bread to eat?"

Preston held up his hands. "Forget the others. You look like an angel. Lady Marian is the best."

"You sure?"

"Yes."

She looked to Marge, who nodded, then to Audrey who confirmed it with a nod of her own then added, "Without a doubt."

He pulled her chair out. "We still haven't seen Natalie's. Have a seat."

Like she'd been hiding in the hall waiting for her turn, Natalie appeared in the doorway with her housecoat draped over her shoulders. She stepped into the room and flipped off the coat, held out her hands, both to the left, then began to wiggle everything.

Preston couldn't make his eyes not look, even though he knew he shouldn't. It had been a long time since he'd seen that much female flesh.

Natalie swished her hips. Her too-short grass-skirt swayed. "What do you think? I'm Princess Liliuokalani—from Hawaii."

He shrugged and managed to avert his eyes. "I don't know. The folks I judged with were pretty conservative."

Vicki shook her head. "Don't listen to him. It's cute."

He stood and nodded toward Natalie's chair. She hula danced her way there.

"You ladies excuse me for a moment."

Marge watched him disappear then faced Natalie. "I'm with Dub, dear. It's too, too much. Maybe you should at least rethink the top."

"Yeah? Well, forget what he said. Didn't you notice he couldn't take his eyes off me?"

Marge wanted to say more but let it drop. Indeed, she'd seen the look on Preston's face, one more of shock than anything. Would he ever cease to amaze her with the depth of his goodness? If only things were different. If only he would forget this stupid game he had them playing.

But that wasn't going to happen, and she knew it. She'd be going home the minute they returned. Stephanie would be standing by for a call when they started back from Jefferson, and Marge could leave before he counted scores and had a chance to send her packing.

The sound of leather soles treading flagstone brought her back from her mental reassurances. Preston, in the silk suit Audrey bought him in Dallas, backed around the corner pulling a metal clothes rack full of something shimmery and shiny.

Audrey jumped to her feet and ran to help him guide the rack into the kitchen. He stopped, grabbed a garment, and held it out. "Capes for my ladies. There's all different colors." He handed the one he held to Marge. "I didn't know what would match, so I had them all delivered. Hope you like them."

Vicki fingered the satin material. Her fingers glided over the silky smoothness like a feather floating on a summer's breeze. "Oh, I love it." She twirled it over her shoulders. "We are going to have so much fun."

"I hope so."

"Why don't you come with us?"

"Not this time."

She slipped the cape's one gold button into its holder, curtsied, then held out her hand. "May I have this dance?"

He bowed then stepped into her out stretched arms. "Of course."

CHAPTER TWENTY-THREE

*Journal entry—June 28*th
  Love it when she uses my basket name, but something's bugging her.

Twice Thursday night, and once more early Friday morning, Marge dialed her daughter's number only to stop before she keyed the last digit. It hadn't been so much the way he danced with her, but the way he held the other ladies that warmed her heart and made her regret her decision to leave.

Even though obvious to everyone except Natalie, the girl's costume—or lack thereof—made him uncomfortable, but he still didn't play favorites. Danced with everyone, even the scantily clad Hawaiian princess though he held her away an extra six inches. But he didn't dance with any of them the way he danced with Marge.

Why had she called Stephanie? Then again, why was he still playing the game? The answer to the first question, she knew. Calling her daughter meant she couldn't back out as easily on her decision. Logic told her she had to be done with all this once and for all—even if it meant losing him.

She zipped her suitcase shut, rolled it to the door, then turned around and studied her room. It hurt her heart that she'd never spend another night there. For a second, she thought about one more call to Stephanie, but she chased the thought away.

"You can't have a relationship based on luck." She said aloud as she closed the door behind her. She rolled her suitcase down the hall chiding herself for being such a baby. She needed to forget about him. If all he wanted was a good-luck girl, he needed someone else.

At the door leading out to the patio, she felt for the light switch, then decided to leave it off—might wake Preston. After all, it wasn't even four yet. She stepped through into the dry heat and checked the thermometer. Almost ninety degrees in the dead of night. This heat wave, she could do without.

"Good morning."

She jumped. The sound of his bass pulled her to the right. He sat in the far patio chair. She smiled. "Actually it's the middle of the night."

"That it is." He held his mug out, the one she'd bought for him in Dallas. "There's more."

She followed him back inside, poured the fresh pot into a carafe, then joined him at the kitchen table. "Well, Buck, how's it going?"

"Almost perfect." He smiled, but not his usual grin. He opened his mouth a bit more than normal and his eyes sparkled extra bright. He looked into her eyes. She forgot to breathe. He leaned closer. She wanted to kiss him, hold and be held by him, but instead, she tore her eyes away and studied a scuffed spot on the stone floor.

"What's the matter?"

She shook her head. Now wasn't the time. "Nothing."

He put his hand on hers. Why did he have to be so discerning? She should've stayed in her room. "But I thought you were excited about going to Jefferson."

187

She looked up. The moment had passed or he had quit smiling. Maybe both. "Oh, I am. We'll have a ball." She nodded. "Thank you very much for the trip."

"You're welcome."

She stared into his eyes, and his smile returned. Oh, how she wanted to smile back but refrained. She wanted so badly to stay with him, never leave his side, but not bad enough to be governed by his stupid rules and the threat of being sent away.

If only he was a control freak or pathological liar, then it would be easier to walk away. But the opposite was true, except for the game. Why did he have to put so much stock in luck? She didn't even believe in it, blessings were from God, not Lady Luck.

He touched her arm. "Penny for your thoughts."

She focused on him. "You don't really want to know."

He chuckled. "Sure I do."

She turned her head and studied her spot again. "No, you don't." She grabbed the carafe. "Want more coffee?"

"Sure." He held out his cup and leaned even closer, his shoulder touched hers. "What's the matter, Marge? What's got you upset?"

"You. Your game. I wish things were different."

"They will be."

She nodded. Yes, they would. "So, we cooking breakfast?"

"Of course. Can't send my favorite ladies out into the mean old world without feeding you first."

Soon he had bacon and sausage slow cooking while she chopped veggies for omelets. Before he finished mixing the biscuit dough, Audrey joined them. As if they had been doing it every day for a year, the three of them whipped out a breakfast fit for royalty without breaking a sweat.

Then the limo came, and it was all over. Marge would

never spend another day under his roof, never get to sip coffee with him in cool of the morning.

The driver paused at the entrance, and she asked the Lord to bless her little garden. The bright yellow, red, and peach daisies waved their heads in a breeze as though saying good-bye. A hard knot of regret grew like a snowball rolling down a hill. It clogged her chest then made its way to her throat. She sucked her lungs full.

A thousand images of him flashed through her mind. That first day when he stood framed in the front doorway, him working in the apple orchard surrounded by their delicate blossoms, and seated at the head of the table. How could she go on without him? For several miles, she stared out the window and wallowed in what-ifs.

The car turned off the farm-to-market onto the interstate. Once the stretched Cadillac merged into traffic and hit cruising speed, she focused on the here and now. She was going to Jefferson, staying at a great old house, and attending a costume ball, never mind all the other fun stuff planned. It would be great, and she determined not to let her decision ruin the trip. She would enjoy herself. Forget Winston Grant Preston. Humph. Someone she used to know. Her new life started today, and he wasn't a part of it.

She resolved to hold that thought, and repeatedly denied him mental access all the way to their bed and breakfast. The innkeeper led her and the other ladies upstairs to deposit their luggage. The massive oak staircase turned midway, then connected to a rather large hall.

"Each of the seven rooms has a different theme and color scheme," the hostess explained as Marge deposited her bags in the closest room. Over a hundred hummingbirds deco-rated its bright garden atmosphere. In no time they all re-turned downstairs for the rest of the tour. She only had to slam the door on him twenty times or so during the fifteen-minute tour of the Hale House.

She loved everything about the wonderful old Greek Revival home of spinster musician May Belle Hale, and he would, too. Oh, phooey, there she went again.

The history of the house fascinated her as did Miss Hale's organ from the early eighteen hundreds. The parlor, dining room, and kitchen furnished with period pieces made it seem like stepping back in time to a more gracious, gentile period.

On the south side, a screened-in porch would be perfect for early morning coffee. The white wicker beckoned thoughts of—No, stop that now. And her guide saved the best for last—the gazebo attached to the north side porch by a covered walk. A lazy ceiling fan blew a constant breeze in the face of the summer heat.

He crept back into her thoughts as she unpacked, but he wasn't there, would never be there with her. This was her adventure with three good girl friends, not him.

A knock pulled her around. "Hey, Lady Bug." Her door cracked opened, and Vicki peeked in. "You ready?"

"For what?"

The younger woman's eyes widened, and she threw her hands up. "Shopping? There's more than a hundred antique shops within walking distance."

Marge started to decline. Didn't really want to go, but she did want to spend time with Vicki, and she may never have another chance. "Sure, let's go."

Vicki waited while Marge changed into tennies then hurried the older woman out. For the first block of the three or so to downtown, Vicki didn't say anything. She hoped her friend would spill her guts on her own, but by the second cross street, it became apparent she wouldn't. "So?" Vicki started then stepped up onto the curb. "You're being too quiet. What's the matter?"

"Nothing, dear. I'm fine."

"No, you're not, not unless you've had your soul sucked out by aliens. Otherwise, yes, something is wrong, and you know how I am. I won't let it go until I know." She wiggled her eyebrows.

Marge laughed, not her usual good humor chuckle, more wry. "Am I that transparent?"

"Lady Bug, you always go around unzipped, that's one of the reasons we all love you so much."

She smiled. "I love you, too."

"So what is it?"

Marge stepped up on the next curb then pointed across the street. "Oh, there it is! It's the library. Let's go have a look."

Vicki let herself be led astray from her self-appointed rounds at the antique shops, but not for long. Like a good friend, she didn't pressure Marge to unload while they explored Carnegie's turn-of-the-century gift to the city, but neither did she completely forget it. Couldn't stop thinking about it.

After the library and a half dozen shops, the answer hit her. She mulled it over before giving voice to her suspicions. On the sidewalk in front of the wonderful old hardware store they'd been cruising, she grabbed Marge's arm and stopped her. "You're thinking about leaving, aren't you?" She held her eyes. "That's it, isn't it?"

Marge looked away. "I have to."

"But why? It's almost over."

"When we get back, it is over for me."

Vicki took her hand. "Don't do this. You'll lose him."

"I never had him, and I can't play his game anymore."

191

Marge shooed a fly off Vicki. "I just can't."

"But you heard him. Probably no one goes home this month."

"Maybe so, but what about the next? There's still four of us—five if you count Virginia."

"Things have changed, Lady Bug. I don't think he wants—"

"Oh, I know he hates it. He even got drunk that first time because he could hardly stand to send Dot away, but he did."

"See? He's changing his rules, to make it easy on us."

Marge smiled. "I'll make it real easy on him. I'm leaving before he counts us up. I couldn't stand being sent home, yet I don't want to stay and watch you or Audrey leave—Natalie, either. You know how fond I am of you, but it still goes all over me every time he calls you darling."

"No, Marge. He doesn't mean—"

She held up her hand, her eyes filled with tears. "Stop. Just stop it right now. I don't want to talk about him or his game anymore. Understood?" She looked both ways then marched across the street leaving Vicki standing with her mouth open. She'd never heard the older woman sound so harsh.

What could she say to make her friend change her mind, make her understand about the relationship she had with Preston? The idea of losing and being sent away bugged her, too, but she always rejected it as though she would stay forever. Wild horses couldn't drag her away. A life without Preston in it was no life. She hurried to catch up. "I sure hope you'll change your mind."

"I can't. Everything's already arranged with my daughter."

CHAPTER TWENTY-FOUR

Journal entry—June 29th
I loved the way the cape wrapped around her when she twirled.

The younger woman kept dropping little openings as they shopped, but Marge never took the bait. She'd already said more than she should. The girl didn't press it after Marge made it clear that she didn't want to talk about it. Forgetting Preston topped her list, then she could put it all behind her. She wished she'd never seen his stupid newspaper ad.

For the most part, the afternoon proved pleasantly entertaining. The Scarlett O'Hardy's Gone With the Wind Museum kept her mind occupied for a spell, and she even went in with Vicki and bought a great Shaker table at Three Rivers Antiques. It would fit regally in the big hall next to the French doors. Shame she wouldn't be there when it arrived, but it was still perfect. He'd love it.

Maybe he would send her a wedding invitation, and she could see it then—if she thought she could stand watching him marry Vicki or Audrey. He surely wouldn't choose Natalie, she was so wrong for him. But maybe Virginia. He might have left that door open because she had been his first choice all along.

By the time for the mystery folks' cheese and wine reception, she was famished. Then after a fabulous meal at Auntie Skinner's, she managed to shove Preston to the back of her thoughts long enough to solve Diamond Bessie's mysterious murder. It tickled her that none of the other ladies did. He would have, but he wasn't here.

That night she resolved to put him out of her mind, but ended up dreaming about skinny dipping with him in the little hidden lake. She told herself she didn't do it on purpose. The next morning while she sipped coffee and waited for the sun, he haunted her thoughts. A thousand times, she thought to call Stephanie and cancel but never picked up the phone. She was leaving. Period. Matter of fact, she was already gone, and he just didn't know it yet.

She indulged in incessant chatter through breakfast and kept him off her mind, and the rest of the morning, only thought about him a half dozen times or so. Lunch with the Pulpwood Queens and meeting all those Texas authors thrilled her. She couldn't remember when she'd laughed more. The women in their leopard and hot pink designs with their rhinestone tiaras were the funnest, wildest bunch she'd ever met. And she got a signed book from each author. All in all, a nice diversion.

But the beauty works later lent too much thinking time. Vicki strutting around in her new jacket and tiara helped some, but even the antics of the newest Queen didn't completely sweep him from her thoughts.

The Queens alone would have fueled several early morning conversations over coffee, but those days were over. She'd never do it again. All because of his irrational, illogical, incomprehensible belief in luck. Well, she'd never been lucky, so that was that. And he was history.

She milked that attitude for the rest of the afternoon, then once it neared time to get ready, the idea of attending her first costume ball overcame her melancholy. Back at the Hale House while she dressed, she remembered Esther's dilemma and decided she didn't have to worry. At least her life wasn't on the line or anything.

On the surface, that logic argued a compelling self-debate, but as she compared other Bible stories, it hit her. Her life—or least what she wanted it be—was on the line. But it would never be a life based on luck. By the time she finished the last minute details, she decided to do as Queen Esther had—put her trust in God. Oh, she'd been praying plenty already, but in the end, trusting Him was all she knew to do.

Shortly, someone tapped on her door, then Audrey peeked in. "Ready?"

With one last look in the mirror, Marge grabbed her cape and followed her friend down the stairs.

One hundred and twenty miles east by southeast, the unseen member of their gaggle was also ready. Thanks to Jorje, his gang of *hombres,* and the boy wonder who looked twelve—but was really twenty-three—Preston's bedroom had been transformed into a command center worthy of an academy award winning spy thriller. Monitors filled every surface.

Tiny hidden cameras with microphones everywhere the ladies would be that night, except their private rooms of course, would chronicle the evening. With a flick of a finger, he could see, hear, and record them through any of twenty-six video-cams. The City of Jefferson had let him tap into two of their new intersection cameras, and Friends of the Library couldn't have been more accommodating after he offered to donate the system to help keep the old Carnegie treasure safe and secure.

The horse-drawn carriage decorated with twinkling lights eased into place three minutes ahead of schedule. Preston flipped a switch and the image of the Hale House's front porch blinked off its small monitor then onto the big screen. Ah, a terrific view from across the street. Well, a leaf bobbed in and out on one corner, but that shouldn't block anything. He leaned back in his chair and waited.

Forty-five seconds later, the door swung open. Vicki led the way in her blue cape, then hot pink Natalie followed by Marge in emerald with Audrey the van guard in red. He loved seeing their excitement. Once in, the driver tapped the horse's rump, and his ladies were off. Preston tracked them to the Library on the three street cameras' tiny monitors, then switched the big screen to the camera focused on the double stairs leading to the second floor ball room.

Heads turned as the four entered. Each signed the guest register then lingered a few feet inside the hall in a cluster. Less than a minute passed before two older gentlemen, both dressed as English Lords, inquired to their well being. Preston watched with detached interest as the women found seats, drinks, and fancy plates of goodies.

The DJ struck up a lively tune, something from the seventies. Preston swept the other monitors. No one seemed to be heading in the ladies direction, then all at once, three men stood at their table asking for a dance.

Marge, Natalie, and Vicki accepted. Audrey seemed somewhat miffed, but one of the Lords from the greeting party stopped beside her. She beamed as he led her to the dance floor.

For the next forty-five minutes, he tried seven cameras on the big screen with fourteen different angles on the picture-within-a-picture feature without ever getting one where he could watch all four all the time. They all danced every dance—mostly with different men. Finally, the DJ took a break. Just watching wore Preston out.

The cycle of fifteen minutes off and forty-five on repeated itself again, then judging time arrived. Preston quit playing with camera angle combinations and put the ladies' table on the larger screen. The span of the room shot moved to one of the small picture spots. Every camera recorded separately, so he could review anything he wanted later.

"Ladies and gentlemen." The Master of Ceremonies spoke in a loud voice from the center of the dance floor. "The judges have made their decisions."

The room's low rumble quieted to a stray cough.

"Second runner up for the Most Original Costume." He held the white card out, leaned back, and squinted. "Marge Winters for her Queen Esther." He held up a white sash.

Marge stood then strolled to the dance floor. The man draped the silky material over her shoulder. Preston clapped with the others, but was disappointed for her that she only got third.

After her applause died down, the emcee called up one of the Lords, the one who'd been dancing with Audrey as first runner-up.

"And now for our winner in the Most Original category." He held both hands up and quieted the murmurs. "Let's give a round of applause to Audrey McLaudin for Betty Crocker."

The cook beamed as she hurried to accept her blue sash. She'd never looked more pleased. Well, maybe about the same as when he bragged on her culinary expertise.

With both runner-ups named in the only other category—Most Authentic—Vicki and Natalie squirmed and fidgeted too much. He was almost certain Natalie's princess wouldn't win anything, about as certain as he was that his little girl would win for her Maid Marian. It could win Most Authentic.

The winner was announced—a woman dressed to the

nines as the Queen of Hearts. Obviously a local. He couldn't help getting hot and wished he were there to tell Vicki what a travesty of justice had been perpetrated. It wasn't right. She had worked hard, and her costume was better than good. She looked devastated.

The emcee quieted the room again with a wave. "We have one more announcement. Please. Please, everyone. We still have our grand prize." He held up a crystal bowl. "And this year, our Best in Show goes to Miss Vicki Truchard for her Maid Marian."

Vicki jumped to her feet squealing and ran onto the dance floor. Preston sprang up as well and gave her a standing ovation. "All right." He'd forgotten about Best in Show. Of course it would be announced last.

Once all the picture takers finished, the three winners returned to their table. At first, neither he nor the other ladies noticed Natalie's absence. They seemed too busy oooing and ahhing over Vicki's crystal bowl. But once they did, he'd already re-ran the tape. She slipped out as Vicki accepted her prize and applause.

The other three hung around after the crowd thinned, but then the carriage came. He watched the Hale House's front door, for better than an hour after the carriage pulled away then shut down the monitors, but continued to record. He'd check the tape in the morning.

CHAPTER TWENTY-FIVE

Journal entry—June 28th
I've got to figure a way out.

The creaking of the old hardwood floors brought Marge out of her uneasy sleep. She glanced at the bedside clock. Three forty-two. From the giggles and un-rhythmic steps, she figured Natalie to be more than tipsy. She wondered where she'd been, but certainly not enough to get up and ask. She rolled over and tried to find sleep again, but it wasn't to be. She tossed and turned for half an hour then decided she rather greet the day sipping coffee than fighting pillows.

She flipped the switch on the pot, scabbed a cup as soon as she thought it wouldn't be too strong, then retreated to the gazebo. While she watched a squirrel scamper atop the picketed privacy fence on the north border, it struck her that in a few short hours, she'd be back at her daughter's house and out of Preston's life forever. She hated the thought, but didn't see any other way.

After another great breakfast, she called Stephanie before she walked out to the limo. Everything was set. She couldn't back out now.

Vicki bumped her knee against Marge's. "So, what do you think his rules are going to be?"

"I don't know."

"Awe, come on. How about you, Audrey?" She scooted to the edge of her seat to lean into Marge and Audrey. "I think us three winning a sash buys us another month."

Audrey smiled. "I think you're right, but now on the other hand—" She nodded toward Natalie who slouched in the corner with her eyes closed. "Maybe it's whoever drank the most or stayed out the latest gets to stay another month."

The Polynesian beauty moaned and stirred. "Don't start in on me. What he doesn't know won't hurt him."

Vicki winked and scooted next to Natalie. "What we don't know will hurt us." She nudged Natalie's knee with her own. "Give it up. Where'd you go and what happened?"

Natalie shook her head. "Back to Auntie Skinners. I just wanted to get myself a good stiff drink. That punch was the pits." She sat up. "There was this guy on a sax. Totally awesome. And from the first note—" She closed her eyes. "I'm here to tell you he was killing me softly with his song. Telling my whole life, you know?" She shook her head. "He did that and more with his music."

"What's his name?"

"Don't know." She gave a quick apologetic grin. "Names never came up."

"So you stayed at Auntie's then came home?"

"Oh no. We left there and went over to one of his friends'. I almost didn't come back at all, but it seemed there might be a scene, so . . ." She held out her hands. "Here I am."

Marge couldn't help asking. "What were you giggling about this morning when you came in?"

Natalie chuckled. "Oh, you know. The booze, the music, running out. I had some good loving, and it'd been so long."

Marge grimaced, but saved her sermon on casual sex. Instead, she scooted around and studied the countryside as the limo sped west. Soon Natalie snored softly in the corner and

Vicki and Audrey started a game of rummy. 'If only' echoed again in her heart, but the dye was cast. Only thing left was to set the bridge on fire.

Preston had their return timed to the minute. With three to spare, he walked out to the patio. The gravel on his lane hadn't been crunched so often since . . . since . . . well, since Nancy died, he guessed, but he sure could get used to all this coming and going. He stopped almost at the exact spot he had stood when they left. The limousine rolled to a stop. Jorje burst through the door carrying a large cardboard box.

"That all of it?"

"Every bit, Boss."

The door opened and he helped Vicki out. "Hi, Dub. Did you miss me?"

"Sure, darling, but could you get on inside." He eased her toward the house as Audrey stepped out closely followed by Marge. "Please, ladies, if you would, I need a minute alone with Natalie."

The three disappeared, and he leaned in and faced her.

She waved and mouthed hi.

"You're fired." He flipped her check onto the seat next to her. "No need to get out. The driver will take you wherever you want to go. Jorje packed up the rest of your things and is loading them as we speak."

"But, Dub. Why?"

He shook his head. "Let's just say I don't care for you coming in at three forty-five in the morning. Never mind you could hardly stand up. No, for sure, you will not be the next Mrs. Preston."

She opened her mouth, but he slammed the door before she could say another word. Once Jorje closed the trunk and let the driver in on the skinny, Preston tapped the roof, and the limo pulled off. He turned around. Marge stood inside the door. He waved her out. "Have a good time?"

She walked to meet him. "It was great."

"Good. Let's go in."

"I can't." She stepped past him and walked toward her suitcase.

"Why not?"

She shook her head and stepped in front of Jorje who carried all the bags. She took hers from him. The Mexican looked to Preston. He nodded, then Jorje continued inside with the other suitcases. She walked toward the lane carrying her bags.

Preston hurried in front of her. "What are you doing?"

She stopped. "Leaving."

"What? But why? You don't have to go." He touched her elbow. "Is this about Natalie?"

She refused to meet his eyes, and hers were brimming with tears. "Heavens no. I just can't play the game any more. I'm sorry, Dub. Truly." A lone teardrop escaped and ran down her cheek. "And yes, I do have to go."

Up the lane, tires displaced thousands of tiny stones, but now the coming and going stabbed at his heart. "But you won."

"No, not me." She sniffled. "I'm not a lucky person, Dub."

A sedan pulled into view then skidded to a stop beside her. A young woman jumped out. She stared daggers.

"Is this the infamous Stephanie?"

"The one and only." Marge waved at her daughter, "Hi, honey," then gestured toward Preston. "Sweetheart, this is W. G. Preston."

The woman nodded.

"Hi, Stephanie. Tell your mother she's making a mistake."

"Sorry. That's not the way I see it."

He sat the bag in the back seat then opened the front door. "Well, I think you're making a mistake, but I won't stop you if you're determined to go."

Marge slipped in, and he eased the door closed. Stephanie cranked the engine to life. He motioned for her to turn around in the drive then stepped across the lane. When the sedan approached on it's way out, he held up his hand. The car stopped, and Marge rolled down her window.

He squatted to eye level. "I lied to you."

"You lied?" Her tears ran freely now. "When?"

"You were the first one I hired, not the last."

She shook her head and swiped at her cheek. "Oh, for goodness sakes, why would you lie about that?"

"Stay, and I'll explain."

She glanced at her daughter then back. "No. No more games of luck and no more lies. Personally, I'm one who guards the truth. I never figured you for a liar, but what difference does it make now if I was hired first or last or in the middle?"

For a split second she seemed to waiver, then she set her face forward. She wasn't going to relent. He pushed himself up. "Have a safe trip. I'll send your money."

She wiped at more tears, but waved for her daughter to drive on. Stephanie shifted into gear and rolled down the lane. He watched until the car disappeared. A rock grew in the pit of his stomach and a heavy weight settled in his chest.

Marge never turned around. How could she leave like that?

He ran after her, but winded before he caught sight of the car again. What was he thinking? He should never have let her go. Once he got a couple of breaths, he walked to the end of the lane, but the farm-to-market was empty.

The cheerfully colored Gerber daisies in the bed she'd worked back to life mocked him. Why'd you let her leave? He waited there by the narrow black-top road until his heart stopped pounding and he could breath through his nose again then gave her another thirty minutes.

She wasn't coming back.

For lack of a better place, he trudged back to the house.

Vicki and Audrey stood on the patio. Without a word, he herded them to the kitchen. "Well, now." He stopped at the head of the table. "Seems to me I've never fired someone then had another one quit me back to back like that."

Neither of the ladies said a word.

He dug in his shirt pocket and pulled out the one page of rules, glanced at it, then tossed it on the table. "Things didn't work out like I planned, but there's the rules if you're interested." He headed for the door.

"What about the game?" He stopped midway and turned around. Vicki arched one eyebrow. "I thought you wanted a wife, and you said you'd decided to marry one of us. Looks to me like pickings are getting slim. So, unless Virginia's coming back, maybe we should just flip a coin."

He chuckled. "We'll talk about it later."

Ironically, Marge had told Stephanie the exact same thing almost as soon as her daughter pulled off Preston's property—minus the chuckle and false bravado. Their conversation covered all the happenings of the last month with the kids and Wayne and most every other small-talk category. Then a silence settled over the little Maxima that lasted for miles.

Apparently Stephanie thought once she reached sight of Dallas' skyline, it was later enough. "You do know who he is, don't you?"

Marge pulled herself to the now. "What, dear?"

"You did know that that was *the* W. G. Preston you were working for?"

"Yes, I knew."

"He's like the richest guy in Texas."

"Oh, he doesn't have Gates kind of bucks, but I suppose he could buy a couple of small countries."

"And exactly what was it again you were doing there?"

"We've already covered that. I signed a non-disclosure agreement. I gave my word."

"Well don't tell me then. Let me guess, and you just nod. So did anyone else stay there I would know? I mean anyone famous."

Marge smiled. She knew her daughter well, and until Stephanie uncovered the whole story, it would drive her crazy, but what could she do? "Sweetheart, I'm not going to tell you what I did, who I met, or anything about my time at the bed and breakfast. It's over. Let's forget about it."

"Okay, fine. Then just tell me why he wanted you to stay so bad?"

"Stephanie, please."

"Oh, Mother. You know I can keep a secret."

Marge didn't bother to respond. Just the opposite was true, but why rehash ancient history? Why indeed when there was so much else to think about—such as what to do with the rest of her life?

Hugging her grandchildren again and her old familiar room soothed her frazzled nerves, but that night, the pain in his eyes when she left tormented her. Deep into the night, her heart bled salty tears of 'what if' and 'why'. If only her head could make her heart understand. A relationship could not be based on luck—or lies. No, all her heart understood or cared about was that he wasn't on the other side of the kitchen.

During one of the few dry spells, a troubled sleep found her, but the respite only lasted until the first whiff of coffee reached her with its bittersweet memories.

That morning, Marge managed to occupy herself with the kids and her old routine, but the higher the sun rose, the more she missed him. Like a lost limb, would he trouble her for the rest of her life? Logic told her no, that time healed all wounds, but her heart refused to hear it.

Then the noon hour arrived. She reminisced, reliving all the anticipation of him coming in from the orchard for lunch. A picture of him and Vicki laughing with Audrey over one of her multiple-course meals troubled her. In her vision, the younger woman acted blatant, more like in the beginning. He smothered her with darlings and the cook with grand compliments.

She'd just about talked herself into a crying jag when the doorbell rang. She choked back tears. No one seemed to hear the bell. The grandchildren remained mesmerized in front of a Rugrats cartoon. Where was Stephanie anyway?

"Coleman?" The five year old didn't budge. "Coleman." He acknowledged her with a quick turn. "Honey, would you answer the door? It's probably one of your friends."

The boy jumped up and ran towards the front door. He barely beat his younger sister Kenzie out of the room. She dogged him hard. The raced ended with the two of them crashing into the living room wall. Marge shook her head and listened, but couldn't hear anything else until the door slammed shut. Shortly, Coleman peeked around the corner into the den.

"Gram, he's for you."

"For me? Who is it?"

The three year old's eyes widened. "He's a stranger." She

made a scared face and shivered.

"Oh, Kenzie, it'll be all right. Don't be frightened. Gram will go see, okay?"

Coleman grabbed his sister's hand and followed Marge back toward the door. "His name's Buck, Gram."

For a split second the basket name didn't register, then she stopped mid-step. Buck? Her mouth went dry, and her heart raced. What would he be doing here? She tried to swallow, but couldn't. How did she look? She fingered her hair trying to bring an errant curl into submission.

Buck? It couldn't be. Coleman must have misunderstood. Preston would never leave his property. Maybe it was Jorje with a message. Maybe something awful had happened. Or maybe he only came to bring her a wedding invitation. Had he decided to get married so quickly that there wasn't time for the mail? Coleman pulled on her skirt and brought her back to reality.

She sighed. Convinced it wasn't him after all, she found her legs and continued to the front of the house with the two little ones trailing close. How silly could she be? She'd know the whole of it soon enough, and she'd live with whatever the news might be.

She opened the door fully expecting Jorje, but W. G. Preston stood on the front porch grinning in all his wonderful glory and decked out in the new silk suit Audrey had bought. She shouldn't have lost so many points for that. His hands were full of lilies and bags of gaily wrapped packages.

"You?" How could he be more handsome than she remembered? Funny how quickly one forgets minute details. She shook her head. "Why did you lie to me?"

His smiled disappeared. "Can I come in?"

She nodded. "I guess so. What are you doing here?"

"Came bearing gifts. Came to rescue the Pretty Woman

from a dreary, loveless life, but you didn't have a balcony to climb."

It was one of her favorite movies. She laughed a nervous twitter. "Are you comparing me to Julia Roberts?"

Stephanie came in with her hair wrapped in a towel. He handed her the flowers and sat down the packages. Coleman yanked her skirt again. "Who is he, Gram?"

"Oh, I'm sorry. Mr. Preston, I'd like you to meet my grandchildren." Marge looked over her shoulder. "And you've already met Stephie."

"Hi." He smiled at her then lowered his gaze. "You must be Master Coleman." He stuck his hand out, but the boy slapped it then held his palm in the air.

"High five," he hollered.

Preston laughed and slapped the boy's palm back. "And this lovely young lady must be Miss Kenzie."

She hid behind Marge's skirt and eyed him with speculative interest.

"Look what I've brought for you, Kenzie." He held out a gift bag filled with pink and purple boxes tied with pastel colored ribbons and bows. She gave him a shy grin and reached for the beribboned handles.

"Hey, where's mine?" Coleman inspected the other bags.

Preston lifted a bag filled with bright primary packages. "This one right here's yours, buddy."

He caught Marge's eye and stared at her while the children tore into the gifts. She still couldn't believe he stood there in her house. He lifted her hand and patted it.

"Had to see you again, Marge. Hold your hand."

She gripped his and pulled him into the den where she sat on the couch and patted the seat next to her. Stephanie followed as far as the doorway. He shocked her by kneeling. What was he doing? Why was he getting on the floor?

"Marge, would you grow old with me?" He retrieved a small velvet box from his suit pocket. "I can't imagine anything that would please me more. I love you, Lady Bug. From that first day. I knew I had to get to know you better. I'd about given up on my idea when you walked into my life." Even though she would've thought there were no more tears to cry, her vision blurred. "I'm sorry I lied to you, but I was so smitten I was afraid you wouldn't agree to come if you'd known you were the first. You were a lot like Nancy. I knew what she would buy at Canton, and I knew what she would buy for me. You scared me a bit at the poker game, but even then, the cream rose to the top.

"I never would have sent you away." He took her hand. "The game was the only way I could think of to be sure a woman loved me and not my money. If I had any doubts at all, your reaction to my giving it away cemented it.

"I love you, and I know you love me." He propped the velvet lid open and extended the box toward her. A heart shaped diamond the size of New Jersey sat high on a band of gold. "Will you do me the honor of marrying me?"

EPILOGUE

Of course Marge said yes. She chose the get-married-quick Reno option, so they only had one week, well, five short days, for personal couriers to deliver the invitations along with round trip tickets and hotel accommodations. Amazing what money can accomplish.

She also said yes to hiring Audrey as chef, and Vicki as HER personal assistant, but only after he promised never to call the young woman 'darling' again. The arrangements thrilled both women.

Only six of the ladies, including Virginia, managed the trip to Reno and served as bridesmaids. It seems Natalie ran off with the saxophone player, and no further effort was made to contact her. The fairytale excited Stephanie so that she could hardly contain herself, but managed to serve as a top-notch matron-of-honor. Jorje, James T., and Wayne stood with Preston.

He consented to the publication of Nancy's article, and it appeared the same day as their wedding announcement. While talking to Susie, he had invited her to tag along to Reno for the exclusive story. Both stories not only graced the front page of the *Dallas Sunday Morning News*, but were picked up and featured across the country.

And yes, they all lived happily-ever-after . . . Until, that is, Preston finally got sick enough of the shenanigans in

Austin to do something about it. The scoundrels and carpetbaggers left him no choice but to run for governor. But then, that's another story.

Journal
of
W. G. Preston

December 25th

Well, finally told Nancy about my plan. Pulled a few weeds while I was there. Cried some, but not much. When I tidied up, it dawned on me I hadn't been for several weeks. Even after all this time, it still hurts, but not like it did. I can't believe it's been five years today.

Funny, that first year I couldn't stay away, now it's hard to go. Maybe time does heal all wounds. I wish she could tell me what she thinks of my idea. Jorje wants me to let him find me a wife. Then again, he also wanted me to marry his cousin, and that would have been a terrible mistake.

Can I ever find someone like Nancy? What a high standard she set.

Oh well, I'm going to do it. Already set things in motion.

January 12th

Got my first batch of applications today. My *amigo* and a couple of his *hombre*s are sorting them out now. Sure hope those jokers don't get the pictures mixed up. Should be an interesting next couple of days.

January 19th

Interviewed Audrey McLaudin this afternoon. Age 44. Honey-blond hair just past her shoulders. She was raised on a sheep ranch near Meridian then spent her adult life in Houston. Texan through and through.

January 22nd

Rained some this morning. Met Vicki Truchard this afternoon. Only 27. Dark hair with blond streaks. Why do women do that? Glamour girl dressed up, but sense a girl-next-door vamp when she's not.

January 29th

Virginia Spencer. Age 46. Finally, someone worth remembering this week. I like her silver hair, especially the way it curls around her face. Ex-ballerina with legs like a thoroughbred. She's quiet and graceful, but not exactly what I'm looking for.

January 31st

Another day wasted. This could be the worst idea I've ever had. On the other hand, I talked to more women just this afternoon than in the last five years. Got to admit, I enjoyed them, especially how they smell. Been a long time.

Well as Scarlett said, tomorrow is another day. I've got the local talent coming, maybe a home-grown girl's what I need.

February 1st

I take it all back. I'm smitten. Her name is Marjorie Anne Winters. Goes by Marge. She's 48 years old, has salt and pepper hair that would look great long, and has been a widow five years.

Do I believe in love at first sight? Smitten for sure, from

the minute I saw her, liked her even more during the interview when she stood up to me over that silly tattoo question. Hired her on the spot, actually I talked her into taking the job.

I lied to her, but didn't think she would have considered my offer if she thought she was the first hired. Even with the big lie, for a while there I didn't think she was going to take the job. Don't know what I would've done. Probably gone to Mesquite and camped out at her house like I use to at Nancy's. Man I wish I could tell her about Marge. She would like her a lot.

Anyway, this is going to be great. The plan is working, I actually hired the first one, and what a lady. Now to find seven more women willing to come before the first of March. Got a whole month, but best be getting busy before Marge finds me out.

February 10th

Second interview for Vicki. Had to think long and hard about hiring this little prima donna. Appears to be a money grubber. Her eyes sparkled extra bright at the mention of the salary and what she had to do for it. There's no way I'd marry this one, but Marge doesn't know that. It'll be fun to see how she reacts to Miss Truchard.

February 12th

Tickled pink Miss Audrey McLaudin accepted my offer today, but she was hiding something. A little intrigue maybe? Interesting and beautiful lady. She thought playing my game would be an easy way to escape her boring life. Plus, she says she's a cook.

February 15th

I couldn't believe it when the words came out of my

mouth, but I offered the deal to this petite, exotic looking young lady named Natalie Bastion. Notes from first interview on January 23rd, age 29. Hair midnight black—long ponytail she twirls a lot. Looks to be of Polynesian decent.

She's a looker, but I have mixed emotions. Oh well, I offered, and she accepted, so we'll just have to see. Why do I keep hiring younger women? Maybe I'm having a mid-life crisis or something. At least she's older than Vicki.

Can't wait until Marge is here.

Four candidates to go, and half the month's gone.

February 17th

Hired Virginia Spencer today. What an exquisite example of femininity. More my type than the last three. If Marge doesn't work out, I could see myself dating Virginia. She'd sure look good on someone's arm.

Anyway, the process is taking too long. At this rate I'll never have all seven before March one.

February 18th

A redhead name of Holly O'Mallister agreed to come to work. If it wasn't for the notes from the first interview on January 11th, I wouldn't have been able to remember her. She's 35 years old, and I wondered at the time if her bright red hair would keep me awake.

Still not all that impressed, but it's getting close to show-time, and my talent pool is shrinking. I shouldn't have quit interviewing after Marge walked into my life, but that's hind-sight, and this short little month is fast running out of days.

Only ten left till showtime, and I still need two more ladies.

February 22nd

Is there somewhere I could go buy some extra days?

I know for sure I should have kept interviewing.

Well, I hired one strictly on accent today. Man, I am getting desperate. You know, If I'd been halfway smart, I'd of videotaped those interviews. How am I supposed to remember fifty different women that I hardly talked to?

But Charlotte's pretty enough to bat 7th.

February 27th

Man, I've been holding my breath. The last four the agency called back for second interviews had already accepted other employment or couldn't be reached. Thought I was going to have to lie again about one of the eight just not showing up.

Then I had them call a lady I interviewed January 12th — Dorothy Casey, and she said yes to the second interview. Reluctantly, I offered, and she accepted the job. She's 38, has dark hair with a silver streak, and claimed to be a 2nd runner-up for Miss America back when, not that I would look it up. Her lips remind me of Rebecca's. How long's it been since I thought of my non-kissin' cousin, anyway?

Dorothy says 'you know' a lot and talks with her hands, but desperate men make desperate moves. She's maybe a little fluffy, but not that bad, and who cares? I'm fresh out of time.

Why'd I ever tell Marge she was eighth? I have come to the bottom of the barrel, but if everyone shows day after tomorrow, I'll have a full house, and Marge will never know I lied. Can't wait to see her again. Hope someday she appreciates all this trouble I'm going to just to get to know her better.

March 1st

Let the games begin. Everyone came in this morning. Got all my ladies together. Thought for a bit my sandpaper might flake out on me, but little Vicki showed at the last minute. And bless her heart, she already has things stirred up, too. *What a piece of work. I figured she'd be fun, but I had no idea how much. She'll rub them all raw before this deal is over.*

What a bonus. Hope Audrey keeps the kitchen all to herself.

Nice new little wrinkle I dreamed up today. Gonna send one home each month, weed out the also-rans. I told the ladies, and of course, Dorothy didn't like it. It'll be interesting to see how Marge handles herself. I think I like her more now than at first blush.

March 2nd

Boy, I can't believe me. I've got to be the biggest idiot ever was. Never should have told Marge my basket name. Wonder if she'll remember? But it probably helped in the end. I think she was ready to march out when she heard about me killing that guy. Will that always haunt me? *After so many years, I can still feel my fist crushing his jaw. Of all the things I've done, I wish I could take that back the most.*

If I live to be a hundred, I'll never forget the look in her eyes when she asked me about killing a man for calling me a name. *Such passion. Looks like I was right, but time will tell. I have been wrong before—though not very often.*

March 3rd

For Vicki being such a night owl, and me liking my coffee early, she did right well this morning. *I never expected it of her. How'd I ever get by when I didn't have rabbits in my life?* She's so cute. Shame she had such a hard time growing up. Wish Marge would've told me what's really going on with Vicki instead of passing it off as female troubles.

March 10th

Marge is so smart. She and Vicki and I played two games of Scrabble, and she won both. I've never been a good loser, but I think it galled Vicki even more.

March 12th

Less than two weeks in, and I'm already sick of Dorothy trying to organize everything—including me. And Charlotte, if that woman got any more obvious, she'd have to jump naked. And what's up with Natalie? I thought she'd participate and be some fun, but she's such an introvert. I hate the way she twirls that ponytail.

I've got to come up with something fair to send the first one home. Sure don't want Marge, Audrey, or Virginia or Vicki going, but I also don't want to be accused of playing favorites. Oh well, it'll come to me.

March 20th

This is so much fun. I think she's falling in love with me, and I know I'm in love with her. At least I think I am. Could I just be in love with the idea of having a wife again? Of all the women I've ever known, including Nancy, Marge stacks up. There's not a situation I can conceive that I wouldn't be proud to introduce her as my wife.

March 30th

While they're gone to Canton—Man, how long's it been since I've been to First Monday? Hear tell it's five times bigger—Anyway, while they're gone, I figure I'll put them in the balance and see how they measure up.

MARGE—What I like is her intelligence and spunk, that she's an early riser and drinks her coffee black, takes her game

218

playing serious, and that certain mischievous smile she gives only to me. I like the sparkle in her eyes, the way she's friends with all the others, and her laugh.

Hmm, dislikes. Maybe that she jumps to conclusions or believes anything she hears, but I can live with that.

VICKI—What I like : her rabbit slippers, her vulnerability though she tries hard to hide it, her youthful energy, the way she plays the queen's part, that she's coming around—big difference in only thirty days.

Dislikes : Too interested in money, a little on the lazy side

AUDREY—Likes : everything she cooks, that she's easy to talk to and a great listener, she's every bit a lady, and will make someone a wonderful wife. Just not me.

Dislikes : her moodiness, not enough pepper in her soup. About to throw my shoulder shaking pepper.

NATALIE—Likes : her petite-ness, just cute as a bug in a rug, the come-hither look that seems so natural in her almond eyes,

Dislikes : she's too quiet, a loner, that she hasn't made friends of any of the other women

VIRGINIA—Likes : the way she moves, her long legs, the way her curls halo her face. Her smarts.

Dislikes : a little too aloof with the other ladies

HOLLY—Likes : her gardening buddy, her exuberance
Dislikes : those enormous awful artificial breasts, I can't believe she had that done between when I hired her and March 1

CHARLOTTE—Likes : her accent, her knowledge of antiques (found out Nancy and I made some pretty good buys), the natural color of her hair

Dislikes : way too fresh

DOROTHY—Likes : the shape of her lips, her smile, her organizational and leadership qualities, the way she cleans

Dislikes : the way she goes overboard trying to organize everything—including me, and her one-upmanship

Well, we counted up, and good ol' Dorothy lost. How wonderfully intuitive Lady Luck is. And I truly did not know red was her favorite color. I should have guessed.

Pleased me that Marge beat them all, but then why wouldn't she? *It surprised me how much I missed her. Longest afternoon I've spent since I couldn't tell you when.* It's got to be love. Absence makes the heart grow fonder. That's what the poets say. Or is it just lust?

March 31ˢᵗ

Oh, my aching head. I feel so bad I even passed up a game of Backgammon with Marge. *How in the world can anybody do that to themselves every day? It's gonna take me years to forget about how bad I feel right now.* I love playing games with her. She hates to lose as much as I do.

Bee man came, then I showed Vicki the warehouses. The little darling tried to extract a promise from me that I almost gave. But the more I think about it, the more I like the idea of being her daddy. Lord knows none of her step-fathers were any kind of example. *Shame I can't change the past, but then she wouldn't be who she is. Maybe I can help shape her future.*

Marge finally called me Buck.

April 10th

Had my first blossom today.

April 14th

Ladies spread a blanket this afternoon and we had a picnic right in the middle of the orchard. What a ball. Everyone was laughing, even Jorje. Had to do a little maneuvering to sit between Marge and Vicki. If Charlotte doesn't cool it, I may have to send her home early.

I love it that Marge is so interested in the orchard. The bloom is a perfect backdrop for her.

April 19th

Man when things happen around here, they happen in a hurry. Talked to Virginia today about her bum knee. Told her I had insurance—another lie—and she agreed to take medical leave. That ought to keep them guessing.

Found out what Audrey's funk's all about. It's so strange what women get upset over.

With Virginia gone, I told them we're going to play some poker. What Marge lacks in experience, she'll recover in intelligence. She's a people watcher. This is going to be a hoot. I'll miss Virginia being around, though. *She's grace personified. I could watch her all day.*

April 27th

Marge and Holly have done wonders with the entrance. I'm so glad they've spruced up Nancy's bed. Really liked Marge's outfit. She looks good in hats. *Got to watch her some today while she was working. I love the way she can focus on the task at hand. Remarkable. I was hoping she'd notice me watching, but she never did.*

April 29th

She's a natural. Oh the fun we could have had plying the riverboat trade if we'd lived a couple of generations before. What a team we could have made. It's almost *déjà vu* all over again, except in reverse. I won Nancy in a poker game, but Marge won me in a poker game. And she had almost the same reaction as Nancy when she found out what her dad and I had done. I love the way Marge stands up to me. It's so good to have a peer. *Can lightning strike twice? Apparently so. What fire.*

It was closer than I thought. Until that last big hand, Marge was the loser. Man, I've got to do better than that, even if it did work out great. I think it's rather telling that the last two hired were the first two to leave. At least I won't have to watch out for Charlotte anymore.

May 3rd

Well, our romance is progressing nicely. All the things she does and her little looks make it appear Marge truly cares about me as a person. I caught her staring today. She looked away fast and blushed a cute shade of rose. But she's so competitive I just hope that she's not caught up in the game, and I'm reading her wrong.

May 9th

Been busy. Maybe I should quit doing so much around here myself. Vicki even chipped in at the warehouse when a couple of *hombres* left for Mexico early. Made me promise not to tell the other ladies she'd actually been working.

May 19th

Okay. Got to think of something. Haven't been able to

come up with anything yet, and it's starting to bug me. Jorje thinks I should have a field day where they run races and jump over hurdles, loser leaves, but that's a little too much.

May 30th

Parting is not sweet sorrow, it's agony. Can't believe I let them go so far for so long. One good thing about this trip is that I've learned beyond a shadow of a doubt that I love her. Wonder what she got me. You can tell a lot by how a woman shops for you. There's no way she's going to lose. I know in my heart, there's just no way.

May 31st

Boy, the feminist came out in Holly. Like I would think it's okay for a wife of mine to go bar hopping. What do they say? *Justice delayed is justice denied. She who tried to win by the sword lost because she wanted to go clubbing in Deep Ellum.*

I almost blew it. *Never should have kissed her.* Can't believe Marge threatened to leave over it, but I think the big dance convinced her to stay. Wish I had a camera when I told them about the Jefferson costume ball. Thought Marge might hurt herself, grinning so big.

I would be surprised if there wasn't royalty in her family tree. What a lady.

I love the way she handled James T. this morning.

Hopefully Vicki can spin whatever information that reporter's stumbled on to. No way is what I'm doing here going to make it to the papers. *In principle, I like the idea of the free press, but sure wish having money didn't put you in the public domain.*

June 2nd

I can see it now. Vicki asking for more grease and Waters not having enough. And the whole time, Vicki's wanting her to talk, but not wanting to make it sound easy. *Dick Tracy only wished he had as much guts. Oh, to have been a fly on the wall.*

June 14th

That Waters gal did a great job. Sent Vicki to ask Marge about leaving. *Hope it doesn't stir anything up, but I want to know.* Didn't bother me at all that Marge saw me crying over Nancy. That's got to be love.

Stuck my foot in my mouth again. Thought Audrey might cry when I told her I couldn't take her up on the restaurant idea. Man, that was a fabulous meal.

June 27th

Showed Marge Nancy's pond today. Even where we were going to build the house. *Had a little twinge, but it was more right than wrong.* Vicki said Marge is going to Jefferson so that little wanting-to-leave fire's out. She sure didn't seem like she wanted to leave this afternoon. She was thrilled when I told her I wanted to give all my money away, but was a little unbelieving when I explained the problems I was having trying to do that exact thing.

Had a great time. Shame I'm not going to Jefferson, but at least I'll get to see them all dressed up. *Jorje called. Said he and the gang had everything wired.* Even went so far as to get signed releases from two-thirds of the city of Jefferson—or at least that's what he claimed. Probably more like five or six folks. It isn't like we'll have cameras set on anything that isn't public. Dallas has cameras on every corner these days.

Big note to self: Send Natalie packing before she gets any more naked. I can't believe that girl.

I liked Marge's reaction to my reaction.

June 28th

Bittersweet this morning. Marge called me Buck again. *Love it when she uses my basket name, but something's bugging her.* I'm glad and relieved she agreed to go, but *I've got to figure a way out.* Don't want the game to come between us.

I'll tell you what, these breakfasts are tasting so good, I'm seriously considering changing my eating habits to include biscuits and gravy of a morning.

June 29th

Stupid TV didn't do Marge justice, or any of them for that matter. Still, she was gorgeous. *I loved the way the cape wrapped around her when she twirled.* Also liked the way she held the men she danced with at arm's length.

I wonder where little Natalie went, but not enough to wait up. I'll check the tape in the morning.

Rules of the Game

CANTON TRIP
+10 for wood or rusty metal
+20 for anything with a cat
-20 for a dog
+30 for anything green
-30 for red
+40 for anything alive
+20 if bought a gift for one of the other ladies
-20 for getting me anything
+30 for item over fifty years old
-40 for anything plastic
+50 if no money spent other than for food
-50 if you have less than ten dollars left

POKER GAME
$500 change-in
Dealer choice and ante
First out or low lady at the time limit goes home

DALLAS TRIP
+20 for all white underwear
-20 for colored underwear or if it's the wrong size
+30 for anything wooden
+40 for quality work clothes

-40 for wrong size work clothes

+30 for leather work boots

-30 if boots aren't size 12

-50 for suit or any formal wear

+20 for a movie

+20 for a game

+20 for anything leather

-20 for anything from a discount store

+25 for fiction books

+10 for non-fiction

-30 for any magazine

+10 for computer software

+60 for visiting (or if none in town, calling) friends or family

+50 for visiting a church or museum

+20 for going to a movie

+10 if it was an Indy

-30 for being in the West End alone

-40 for being in Deep Ellum by yourself

-30 for being in any bar

-25 for bungie jumping, racing cars, or bowling

JEFFERSON TRIP

To get another month, all a lady has to do is:

Solve the Mystery

-or-

Purchase an antique for the house

-or-

Join the Pulpwood Queens

-or-

Win any place, any category at the costume ball

Author Bio

High school sweethearts, Ron and Caryl McAdoo discovered writing together in the 80s. Accomplishments include two non-fictions, GREAT FIREHOUSE COOKS OF TEXAS and ANTIQUING IN NORTH TEXAS, both from the Republic of Texas Press, a thriller titled THE THIEF OF DREAMS from Longhorn Creek Press, a mystery ABSOLUTE PI due soon for audio release from Books In Motion, and now THE APPLE ORCHARD BED & BREAKFAST.

They both serve on the board of the DFW Writers' Workshop, Ron is president, and are members of the Greater Dallas Writers' Association.

The McAdoos love family get-togethers, messing with their horse herd, travel, and gardening. Plenty of gathering opportunities arise with their children and nine of eleven grandchildren living in the same Irving neighborhood. The lifetime Texas residents give credit for every good blessing to their relationship with Jesus Christ.